OTHER DELL YEARLING BOOKS YOU WILL ENJOY

SOLDIER MOM, *Alice Mead*

WAITING FOR THE RAIN, *Sheila Gordon*

YEAR OF IMPOSSIBLE GOODBYES, *Sook Nyul Choi*

UNDER THE BLOOD-RED SUN, *Graham Salisbury*

WHEN MY NAME WAS KEOKO, *Linda Sue Park*

THE TEARS OF THE SALAMANDER, *Peter Dickinson*

RUNT, *Marion Dane Bauer*

HALF AND HALF, *Lensey Namioka*

TROUT AND ME, *Susan Shreve*

TRUE BLUE, *Jeffrey Lee*

DELL YEARLING BOOKS are designed especially to entertain and enlighten young people. Patricia Reilly Giff, consultant to this series, received her bachelor's degree from Marymount College and a master's degree in history from St. John's University. She holds a Professional Diploma in Reading and a Doctorate of Humane Letters from Hofstra University. She was a teacher and reading consultant for many years, and is the author of numerous books for young readers.

YEAR OF NO RAIN

YEAR OF NO RAIN

Alice Mead

A DELL YEARLING BOOK

*The author gratefully acknowledges Dr. Steven L. Burg,
Adlai E. Stevenson Professor of International Politics, Brandeis University,
for his critical reading of the manuscript.*

Published by
Dell Yearling
an imprint of
Random House Children's Books
a division of Random House, Inc.
New York

If you purchased this book without a cover you should be aware that this book is stolen property. It was reported as "unsold and destroyed" to the publisher and neither the author nor the publisher has received any payment for this "stripped book."

Copyright © 2003 by Alice Mead

The jumping horse design is a registered trademark of Random House, Inc.

All rights reserved. No part of this book may be reproduced or transmitted in any form or by any means, electronic or mechanical, including photocopying, recording, or by any information storage and retrieval system, without the written permission of the publisher, except where permitted by law. For information address Farrar, Straus and Giroux, 19 Union Square West, New York, New York 10003.

The trademarks Yearling and Dell are registered in the U.S. Patent and Trademark Office and in other countries.

Visit us on the Web! www.randomhouse.com/kids

Educators and librarians, for a variety of teaching tools, visit us at
www.randomhouse.com/teachers

ISBN: 0-440-42004-0

Reprinted by arrangement with Farrar, Straus and Giroux

Printed in the United States of America

January 2005

10 9 8 7 6 5 4 3 2 1

OPM

For the children of South Sudan

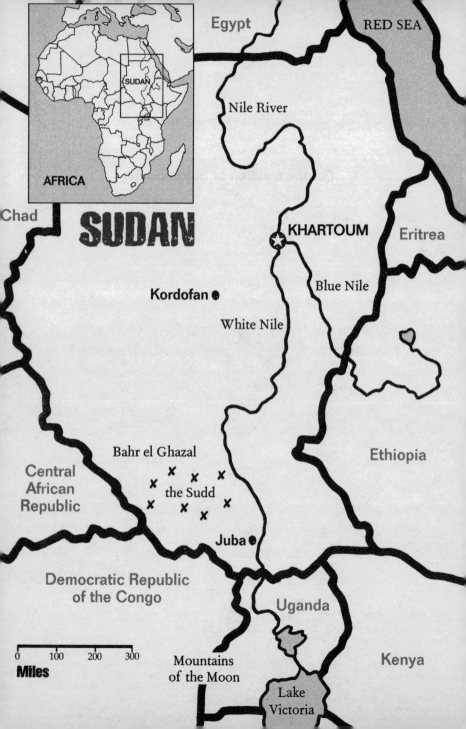

Introduction

Since the end of the Cold War (1989), according to the International Red Cross, there have been fifty-six wars around the world, creating 17 million refugees and 26 million people who have lost their homes.* Many of these wars—in Rwanda, Sierra Leone, Bosnia-Herzegovina, the Congo, Afghanistan, and Somalia—are civil wars.

One of the longest of these modern civil wars has been going on almost continuously since 1983 in the vast African country called Sudan. Before World War II, Sudan was a British colony with separate British administrations in the North and South.

North and South Sudan are very different from each other. The North is hot, dry desert much like Egypt

*William Shawcross, *Deliver Us from Evil* (New York: Simon and Schuster, 2000).

and has a predominantly Muslim population. The South is more diverse both geographically and culturally. It is composed of dry grasslands, a large swamp called the Sudd, and, in the southernmost regions, forested hills. The South is populated by many tribes, including the Dinka, the Nuer, and the Shilluk. Among the South Sudanese are Christians, some Muslims, and people who hold traditional beliefs. Under British rule, the South remained economically disadvantaged and underdeveloped.

Civil war between North and South first broke out shortly after Sudan gained its independence from Britain and was made a single state. There was a brief period of peace in 1972, soon followed by renewed fighting. Then, in 1989, a despotic Islamic military front seized control of the government and has fought ever since to suppress the southern rebel forces and to convert the entire country to the Muslim religion.

Since 1983, an estimated two million Sudanese civilians from villages in the South have died and four million have been made homeless, not only from the fighting, but also from the social chaos, famine, and lack of medical care that have followed. People die of such diseases as malaria and sleeping sickness. Thousands try to escape the soldiers' raids by walking for weeks and even months across deserts and grasslands, through forests and over mountains, to refugee camps in Ethiopia, Uganda, the Central African Republic, or Kenya, or by heading north to Muslim-ruled cities.

Further difficulties are caused by divisions among the Southern rebel forces along tribal lines. The Dinka tribe has fought the Nuer tribe, for example. What's more, soldiers flagrantly disregard human rights, stealing humanitarian food aid, rampaging through villages, destroying cattle and crops, burning homes, and, worst of all, killing or kidnapping civilians. Many of the displaced people who walk from camp to camp are unaccompanied children, either orphaned or separated from their families by the war. Thousands of children are sold as slaves.

Over the years, seventeen rounds of peace talks have failed to stop the war in Sudan. In November 2001, the United States initiated new efforts to bring relief aid to the suffering refugees. Diplomats began working with the northern government on a new peace plan.

This story does not attempt to represent the full scale of this enormous regional and political problem. Instead, it simply portrays one boy's life after his village is attacked, his displacement and his desire to return home.

The people of Sudan, particularly in the South, which I know best, are vibrant, with lots of pride, fond of jokes, and smiling, hauntingly beautiful in their singing. But in the fifteen years of this phase of Sudan's war, they have known more suffering, terror, and death than any other population on earth.

—Roger P. Winter, Executive Director, U.S. Committee for Refugees
(*Sudan: Personal Stories of Sudan's Uprooted People*, 1999)

YEAR OF NO RAIN

One

"**There's a full moon tonight**," Naomi Majok said to her younger brother, Stephen. "And that means a dance!" She pulled him to his feet, dreamily closing her eyes and swaying.

Naomi and Stephen lived with their mother in the Bahr el Ghazal region of southern Sudan, in a small, out-of-the-way village, surrounded by mile upon mile of vast grasslands.

"Uh-oh, Naomi! You're in love!" crowed Stephen. "Who is it? Old Peter Garang? I know—you want his cows. He offered us five for your bride price. We'd be practically rich!"

"Stephen! Of course it's not Peter Garang. He has only three teeth! Anyway," she said, "Wol's mother has ten cows. I know she could match Peter's offer."

"Wait a minute! What are you saying? Wol's interested in offering us a bride price for you? He's just a boy! He's fourteen! Only three years older than I am!"

"Don't tease. I know he's young, but imagine me as Peter's third wife."

"Yes, but he belongs to the most influential family in the village. They have twenty cows!" Stephen said. "Naomi, be serious. Did Wol really make Mama an offer for you?"

"Not yet. But he's going to. At least, I think he will. What do you think? Would he be a good husband for me?" Naomi asked.

Stephen burst out laughing. He couldn't imagine it. He and Wol and Deng, who was thirteen, worked and played together all the time. He couldn't picture Wol and sixteen-year-old Naomi married.

"Stop laughing!" Naomi cried.

"Okay, okay." Stephen cleared his throat and tried to settle down. "Being married to Garang would be awful. And since both families could offer us a price of five cows, the offers are equal. So that means it will be up to Mama to decide."

"Oh, don't say that," Naomi moaned. "That's just the problem. She's sure to choose Garang because of his position in the tribe. And listen, I don't want you to say anything about this to Wol today. Promise?"

"Calm down, Naomi."

"You think this is easy? In three or four years, you may be in the same position."

"Me?" Stephen looked at his sister, surprised. He would never be married. He would study in Egypt or Kenya or who knew where and become a teacher.

At that moment, their mother entered their tukel, a round hut made of mud and grass, with a cone-shaped roof. She was carrying two calabash gourds filled with water from the well. She set them on the dirt floor and rubbed the small of her back.

"There's going to be a dance tonight, Mama," Naomi said.

"Is that so?" her mother said.

She glanced at the mattock leaning against the wall by the entrance. The tool was for digging, for chopping at the dry ground and loosening it. The tarnished blade was bound to the wooden handle with a long cord.

"Naomi," she said sharply, "never mind tonight. What about the crops? Do you expect us to eat weeds? And, Stephen, you boys didn't fix the thorn hedge around the cattle pen yesterday. Three cows disappeared last night. Now you'll have to go looking for them."

Stephen made a face. He, Wol, and their friend Deng had all made new spears yesterday, while watching the cattle. Late in the afternoon, when the heat eased a little, they had thrown their spears at the round gourd they used as a ball until their shoulders ached. So when they brought the cattle back to the village, none of the boys had wanted to repair the thorny branch fence that kept the cows safe overnight.

Acacia thorns were long and sharp and left deep, bloody scratches on the boys' hands and arms. The branches were the cows' only protection against predators. There was always the danger of attack by wild animals, maybe lions, hyenas, or leopards. And the villagers depended on their cows for everything—they drank the milk and blood and burned the dried dung when no firewood could be found.

Stephen thought about the difficulties of dragging more branches to the fence. Still, when their mother ordered them to work, they obeyed. The children quickly hurried out of the tukel.

Sudanese children learned early to work hard for their families. Girls always worked in the home and the fields, struggling to keep the sorghum and maize alive and growing through the terrible heat and what now seemed to be their third year of drought in a row. Boys herded the cattle, which were the pride of all Dinka tribes in the region of Bahr el Ghazal, the River of Gazelles.

It was Stephen's job to take their two cows, a rangy

white one with long curved horns and his favorite, their old yellow cow, from the large pen and out to pasture with the rest of the village cattle. Wol and Deng, the only other older boys in the village, went with him.

Stephen walked across the circle of cone-shaped huts, past the village well, to the cow pen. He saw the tips of the cattle's wide-spaced horns, visible above the thorny branches. One of the old men, dressed in a cloth fastened at the shoulder, was using a long stick to refashion the branches so they would block the hole where the cows had escaped during the night.

Peter Garang watched. He had twenty cows, more than anyone in the village, although once people had had many more. He shouted to Stephen, "Look at this hole! This fence is no good. If you boys did your work properly, my cows would never have gotten loose."

Oh no, Stephen thought. Why couldn't the missing cows belong to someone else?

"Maybe your cows couldn't sleep well last night. The cows want to stay awake when there's a full moon, just like the rest of us, uncle," Stephen said, trying to pacify the old man. "Don't worry. We'll find them."

"Huh. I doubt that," Peter said in disgust, spitting a stream of tobacco juice in the dirt.

Making sure that the children did their work and

minded their elders was the job of all the adults in the village, not just the parents. Peter had a right to criticize the boys. Stephen didn't want Peter to beat him with his stick, so he tried again to change the subject. "There's going to be a dance tonight."

"And your sister needs a wealthy husband," old man Garang said. "She's always singing love songs out in the fields. I hear her. We all hear her. Maybe I'll marry her myself, eh? I've made my offer. When is your mother going to make her decision?"

"I don't know. Soon, I think."

"Your sister is a little too full of herself," Peter Garang said, his dignity somewhat injured.

Stephen stifled a laugh. Naomi was proud of her beauty. And he was sure that she would never marry a snoopy old man like Peter, no matter how many cows he had or what Mama said. Stephen carefully pulled open a place in the thorn fence that served as a crude gate. He used a long pole to pry apart the branches, avoiding the thorns.

As the cows ambled through the opening, Stephen quickly scanned the herd to see which three were missing. The other yellow cow. A white-and-tan one. And a white one with one short horn. It was true. All belonged to Peter Garang.

"See? What did I say? It's only my cows that are

gone. That's no accident, I can tell you. I bet someone did this to me on purpose, thinking, Well, Garang is old, he won't miss them. Ha. If you boys don't find my cows immediately, you can all expect a lashing."

"Yes, uncle."

"Maybe the person who did this to me is the person who wants to offer a bride price for Naomi himself!" shouted Peter.

Stephen hurried the cows toward the grassy open field, where they would graze. He didn't want to be punished on the night of the dance. And it wasn't fair that he had to get the cows alone, that Deng and Wol were late. But maybe that would turn out well. They would owe him a favor in exchange for their lateness. He would send them to look for Peter's cows.

Then Stephen saw his friends, each dressed in a pair of worn shorts, fooling around near the open-sided hut where the village children had had school last year. The teacher had left when the northern soldiers moved into the region.

Deng and Wol were practicing hops and high leaps in the air, their legs tucked under them. They were getting ready for the dance.

"Hey! Never mind that," Stephen shouted. "Come on. You're late! Some cows escaped last night. Now you'll have to go find them!"

Two

Midday on the dry savanna, it was hot. Stephen yawned. Watching cows all day every day was sometimes very, very boring, especially today, with his two friends out searching for the old man's missing cows. To pass the time, Stephen decided to make a second spear, longer and sharper than the one he'd made yesterday. He poked about in the bushes until he found a straight branch, and broke it off. He had a little pocketknife with him that had once belonged to his father. So he sat in the grass and began to sharpen one end of the stick.

He listened to the endless whirring of the locusts in the grass. The herd was small now because of the years of drought. Peter Garang used to have thirty cows. But many had died of drought and starvation, and when that happened, squawking, bare-necked vultures with their ugly dark feathers came to pick the bones.

Oh, well. That was life. His mother said there were often droughts in Sudan. Death was always near. Never mind. They were all in God's hands. Stephen sang songs to himself while he whittled.

Tonight everyone would be singing, teasing Naomi and his family about their search for her husband.

He would be expected to sing some songs, too. He tried to make one up.

The moon is bright on dancing night,
when girls so like to smile.
Naomi's smile, the prettiest one,
is nicer than the rest.
And Peter's cows have wandered off,
and Wol's cows are healthy and young.
But don't worry. Naomi will marry the strongest man,
the one who leaps the highest.

It wasn't a great song, but it didn't have to be. When the time came, he just had to be ready with something funny and teasing to sing.

Dancing nights were rare now, but they were the best times in the village. Everyone loved to sing and joke. The fires burned brightly, red and gold sparks leaping up to the stars. During the dance, the villagers forgot the drought, the war, their hunger.

It did absolutely no good to worry about these things. Everyone said that. Stephen's mother said the endless war was like a plague of locusts that came to the village time after time. There was nothing they could do about it.

The raiding soldiers came and went, stealing food and looking for recruits. The villagers had dug several tunnels away from the circle of huts to hide the children so they wouldn't be captured and forced to become soldiers or be sold as slaves.

Stephen's father had become a soldier. He had gone away to fight when Stephen was a baby and had never come back. Maybe he was working in Khartoum now. Maybe he wasn't a soldier anymore. Maybe one day he would return with a lot of money, money to buy cattle and to send Stephen to boarding school in Egypt.

"Stephen! Hey, Stephen! Hurry!"

He heard Deng calling as he ran across the pasture toward him.

"Yeah? What?" Stephen stood up and shaded his eyes against the glaring sun.

"Come on. We found Garang's white cow. She's dead, dragged under a big thorn tree. A lioness got her. The other two cows must have run away in fear."

"Oh, no." Stephen jumped up and ran after his friend.

"Look!" called Deng. "You can see the buzzards circling from here."

There were the remains of the carcass, near a thicket of thorny bushes. Vultures circled watchfully overhead, disturbed from their meal by the boys.

"Oh, no," Stephen moaned again when he saw the bones. "Now Peter will be even angrier. He thinks the hole in the fence is our fault, and he said he'll lash us if we don't return his cows."

The boys stood silently, regarding the carcass of the dead cow. The loss of a cow was serious, and now they would have to make some kind of payment to Garang.

"Maybe he'll make us each give him one of our cows," Deng said. "As long as we offer payment, he can't punish us."

"That's not fair, Deng. Wol has ten cows and you have six, but we have only two. We can't give him one."

Again the boys were silent, wondering what to do to avoid a beating.

"You know what he's like. He's always plotting something. Maybe he planned this somehow," Wol said at last, scratching a mosquito bite on one of his long, thin legs. "Maybe he made that hole in the fence just so that he can demand payment by taking your cows, which are younger and better than his."

"That doesn't make sense," said Deng. "I bet what he's thinking is that if he lost some cows because of Stephen, then Stephen's mother will have to accept his offer for Naomi."

Stephen and Wol thought this over. Deng was very clever. And what he said had the ring of truth in it. Stephen remembered how Peter had teased him this morning, saying he would marry Naomi.

"Do you think so?" Stephen asked finally.

"Maybe. Who discovered the hole? Peter Garang. Whose cows out of all the cows are the only ones missing? Garang's. Why is that?"

Stephen sank down in the grass. To lose one of their cows to Peter in repayment would be terrible. The cows barely gave any milk in the drought. And it was hunger that made people suspicious of one another. But forcing Naomi to marry old Peter was unthinkable. His mother would never agree to such a thing. Would she?

The bright sunlight danced and shimmered before Stephen's eyes. The white ribs of the freshly killed cow wavered in the grass before him. Flies swarmed and buzzed loudly around the few scraps of meat that still clung to the bones.

The heat made the air quiver. Heat played tricks

with your eyes. Little silver patches of water seemed to glimmer like a path of watery stones all the way to the horizon.

"I have to get back to the herd," Stephen said finally. "You have to keep looking for Peter's cows. And you better find them."

"This wasn't our fault, Stephen," Deng reminded him.

"Yeah, I know." He walked off, trailing his new spear in the dirt behind him. He wanted to find a nice patch of shade so he could rest.

There. Perfect. He lay down beneath a mimosa tree. The ground under his back was hard, hot, and dry. The earth was like dust this year. It was mid-May, and the rainy season should have started by now, but no rain had come at all. That was another reason the villagers' nerves were on edge. Stephen's mother seemed to do little else all day besides scan the sky for clouds.

Often at sunset, they did see clouds gather along the low, forested hills that lay to the south. But after a few brief spatters of raindrops fell, poking holes in the hard-packed dusty ground, the clouds vanished, pulling apart into nothing, like shreds of soft torn cotton. Unless the cloud pattern changed, this would be the third year of no rain. And it wouldn't be just cows who starved. The villagers were so weak and tired, even the adults. And everyone got sick often. Deng's father had died of sleeping sickness the year before.

In the field, Naomi's sorghum plants were small and wilted, barely alive. The corn had sprouted, but that was all. They had no way to irrigate. Two weeks ago, Deng's two aunts took their children and set off in search of a relief center, to beg for an airdrop. They would need a food drop by airplane—sorghum, powdered milk, malaria medicine—to survive till it rained again. The way things were now, the youngest children couldn't last much longer.

Three

It was early afternoon by the time Deng and Wol wandered back to the mimosa tree where Stephen was resting. Peter's lost cows trailed behind them. Deng turned and beat them on the rump with a stick, urging them back into the herd with the others.

"Whew, it's hot," Wol said, dropping to the ground next to Stephen.

The three boys lay quietly in the overpowering heat, watching the cows' tails swish pesky flies off their backs. Locusts whirred in the tall, dry grass. A hawk drifted in high circles in the cloudless blue sky.

Stephen was sure there would be no rain today. But he shouldn't be worrying about rain right now. There was still the terrible problem of Peter's dead cow. The problem seemed insurmountable. If they had to give up one of their cows in payment, his mother might lash him. And Peter might beat him if they didn't.

"Stephen," Wol said suddenly, "do you think Naomi likes me?"

"You? I don't know," Stephen said carefully. "But she mentioned you today, so I think she does."

"Yeah? I was thinking . . . maybe I'll tell old Garang that she likes me. That she will marry me."

Stephen sat up. "But why, Wol?"

"Because. Think about it from my side. I want to marry soon." Wol lowered his voice, even though they were far from the village huts. "I want to join the rebel army, but before I leave I want to be married. I want to leave a family in case . . . in case . . . I don't come back."

Stephen's thoughts spun in confusion. What was Wol saying? That he was ready to fight against the heavily armed North, with its planes and bombs? That he was ready to become a father?

"Do you really mean that?" Deng asked.

"Would I tease about something so serious?" Wol asked. "In fact, I will offer five cows, just like Peter."

"Maybe since you're both so young, you should just get engaged to Naomi," Deng said reasonably.

"Yeah, that's a much better idea," Stephen said. "Then you could come back one day and marry when you are both older."

"Stephen, I want you to talk to your sister for me.

We can't allow her to marry Peter Garang, right? So this is the best way. Otherwise your mother will force her into that bad marriage."

Stephen nodded. Wol was a good friend. "Sure, Wol. I'll do it."

"Go now, then, and tell her while she's still in the fields so your mother won't hear about it first. We can manage these lazy old cows without you."

He found Naomi with her two friends, Teresa and Constance, slowly weeding the rows of sorghum, their backs bent. They swayed and sang about dance night and who was beautiful and who was not.

"Naomi! Come over here a minute," Stephen whispered.

She glanced at him fearfully. "What is it? Soldiers?" she asked.

"Ssssh," said Stephen. It was hard to keep any kind of secret in a village. Now the girls would notice that he and his sister were whispering together. Even such a useless bit of information would fly from hut to hut.

"There could be a big problem about your marriage offer," Stephen said. "We think old man Garang tore a hole in the thorn fence and let his cows wander off on purpose. And one died, killed by a lioness. Now he'll tell Mama that this was my fault. And you'll have to accept his offer, to keep the peace."

Naomi stared at Stephen in horror. To have to marry a sneaky old man like Peter Garang and not someone she could grow to love! "This is all so crazy. I won't do it. I'll run away," she said. "I can't marry him. Even if he offers twelve cows, I won't do it."

"You can't run away," Stephen said. "Where would you go?"

"North?" she suggested. "To Khartoum?"

"Come on, Naomi. You can't do that. Listen, Wol also thought about this. And he sent me to ask you—he offered to become engaged to you. That way you can't marry Peter. You can say you have already been secretly engaged for one year."

"Wol suggested this?" she asked. "Or did you put him up to it?"

"Wol offered. I swear."

Naomi smiled.

Teresa and Constance straightened up, watching.

"Naomi, come on. We have to finish this row," Teresa called. Stephen knew the girls didn't care at all about the sorghum but were dying of curiosity.

"In a minute!" she called back.

"Tell him yes, then," she said. "He should say that we have been promised to each other for a year. Here. Give him my coral beads."

She slipped off her necklace of beads and handed it to her brother.

Stephen nodded. "Who will tell Mama?" he asked.

"I will," she said. "You don't need to get mixed up in this. You're still a little boy, right?"

She gave him a quick, hard hug, and with long strides crossed the sorghum field to work beside the others.

That afternoon, when Stephen reached his hut after putting the cows back inside their pen, he heard his mother's voice, quiet but insistent, and he knew she was talking to Naomi about the engagement. He entered the dark tukel, glad to be out of the sun's rays.

"You arranged this behind my back? Now how can I face Peter Garang or his wives? We owe him payment for the dead cow. And what do I have to give? One of ours? Then we will have only one cow," his mother said as she ground grains of sorghum with a mortar and pestle for kisra bread. "You seem to have forgotten that part."

"Mama! Am I not worth one cow to you?" Naomi cried out. "Besides, Wol will give us five."

"Hush! Someone will hear you."

Her mother ground the sorghum to a fine flour and poured it into the kettle filled with well water. Then she scooped out another handful of grain from the sack and began to grind it.

"We will both run away if you force her to marry old Garang," Stephen announced.

"Oh, Stephen." His mother glanced at him and smiled. "Here, take the gourd and go to the well. Hurry up."

Dragging his feet, he picked up the empty calabash. He knew his mother was just trying to get rid of him so she could talk to Naomi without interruption.

"How can Wol marry you? He's a boy still, like Stephen," his mother continued.

"He's fourteen," Stephen said. "And at least he cares about Naomi and how she feels. At least he thought of how she would feel marrying that liar, Garang." He raised his voice. "Which is more than you are doing!"

"Go, I told you. And anyway, how do you know why Wol said that? How do you know that he doesn't want to marry her only because she is beautiful, because then people will speak well of him? What if she becomes ill and loses her beauty? Will he take a second wife? A third? He's young, and we don't know his character yet."

Stephen didn't know what to say. He wanted to argue that Wol was loyal and loved Naomi. But he had no proof.

"Go on. I need the water, Stephen. For cooking. Go before I lose my temper!"

The village huts were spread out in a wide circle around the well. Tended by one of the smaller boys, a cow in a wooden yoke circled the well. The cow walked like that for hours to bring up drinking water from deep in the earth.

When Stephen returned with the heavy gourd, the conversation was over. Naomi was grinding beans, and his mother had started the cooking fire on the ground outside the hut. Neither was speaking. So Stephen stayed silent, as well. It was important to keep peace whenever possible. Who knew what would happen next?

Four

Now the sun began to sink in the west. The sky blazed with streaks of orange and red. Shadows, which had been round black pools at their feet in the early afternoon, slowly lengthened. Stephen, his mother, and Naomi washed their hands and dried them before eating.

They were quiet, still thinking about the cow that had been killed and how that would affect the village.

There were only three people left in the Majok family now. Two younger boys had died, one of malaria, one of diarrhea. Their father had left to fight and never returned. With just two cows, they had little status, little power in the village. To anger or embarrass old Peter at the dance would have long-lasting consequences among all of the Garang relatives and friends.

They sat on their mats, each with a piece of kisra

bread and well water to drink. The beans were still bubbling in the pot on the cook fire just outside.

"Now. We will discuss this calmly. So, Naomi, what do you feel about Wol?" their mother said. "At least you have a choice."

"A choice? Between a man of sixty and a boy of fourteen?" Naomi said bitterly.

"That's more of a choice than many girls have, believe me."

Naomi didn't speak. Then she said, "I like Wol and I do want to be married. But I also want to go to school."

"School? You? A Dinka girl of sixteen? Don't be silly. No teacher will come here, and I can't send you to school in the North. The Muslims would sell you as a slave, and you know it."

"But if I don't go to school, we'll be poor forever. I'll end up on my knees, cooking over a fire, hauling water, chopping weeds all my life. Like you!"

Her mother looked hurt by this, and Naomi began to cry, sniffling as she tore off pieces of bread.

Stephen felt terrible. "I'll go to school, Naomi. I'll study hard and then teach you everything."

His sister gave him a grateful look. But their mother seemed not to hear.

"It's settled, Naomi. I have decided. You can have a

long engagement, until Wol is fifteen or sixteen. Then you can marry. Stephen, go tell him and his mother to come. We must do this, I'm convinced, and we must do it before Peter catches wind of anything. We must not injure his pride any more than we have to."

Bright and clear white over the black landscape, the moon rose swiftly in the east. How fast the moon traveled compared to the big hot sun. The land was so dark that, even with a bright moon, the Milky Way looked like a handful of dusty grain tossed across the sky.

In the center of the village, the bonfire, banked with charcoal and branches, sent up crackling flames to the rhythmic beating of drums. Standing outside the main circle of adults, Deng, Stephen, and Wol wore anklets of jingling tin disks, just like the men. They practiced their leaps and dance steps. Wol was showing off, trying to attract Naomi's attention.

Naomi stood in a group with her friends. Judging by their giggling, Stephen felt sure she had told them about becoming engaged to Wol.

Meanwhile, the older men danced, holding their long spears, casting fantastic shadows in the flickering firelight. Even Peter could still leap high in the air. Like a gazelle!

Then Stephen's mother came for Wol. She took his

arm and pushed him into the circle to dance and leap with the older men, while the women watched and began to gossip.

"Oooooh, Wol!" the women called out. "A man already?"

Wol grinned at them, proud that he was engaged to a beautiful girl and that Naomi had chosen him over Peter. His mother, Mary, dressed in a colorful wraparound skirt, came to greet Stephen's mother while everyone watched. "We are happy to welcome Naomi into our family," she said.

Then Wol's mother led some women in a song, saying that Naomi wanted only the youngest man because she was so beautiful. She deserved the youngest, the one who would outlive her.

After that, Stephen stepped forward and sang his song. And when he mentioned both Peter's and Wol's cows, the whole village clapped loudly and laughed. Everyone knew exactly what had happened that day between the families. And by singing and joking about it all, Stephen had helped the matter to release its angry hold on people's hearts.

The men and women of the tribe all nodded at him as he finished singing, at his choice of words, at his lack of anger. They were pleased that such a young boy could lead them in setting this problem aside.

Stephen smiled at his mother, both knowing that he had done well.

Now he sat at the edge of the circle, watching the flames, listening to the drumming. The moon rose higher, seeming to become smaller as it climbed well above the horizon, the white circle speckled with silvery shadows. He was thankful for Wol, his friend. And for Naomi, his sister. And for his mother, for listening to them. He hoped his village would stay just as it was forever.

Five

After the moonlight dance, the hot days again rolled slowly by like a big wheel that went nowhere. June came, and no rain fell. The crops withered in the dusty field, their leaves turning crisp and brown. And when the wind blew, it sent twisting spirals of dust whirling through the village, coating everything as they spun by.

Peter Garang and his wives now avoided the Majok family, insulted by Naomi's rejection of his offer, and by her choosing Wol, a young man whose character was not yet formed. Peter told everyone in the village that the Majoks had behaved unreasonably toward him and that they owed him an apology. He added that they owed him a cow, or some other compensation for his loss. But no one liked Peter, and no one supported him. So the debt was never paid.

Stephen's mother blamed the bad mood in the village on the drought. The grass was brown, and where the cows walked every day in search of grass to eat, the ground turned to trampled dust, so that if it did rain, the paths and tracks they made would become clogged with deep mud. Only the locusts seemed happy.

Then one day in mid-June, early in the morning, the villagers awakened to the droning sound of a low-flying airplane. Everyone rushed from the huts. Stephen's mother carried a long, bright orange scarf as she ran to the fields. Deng's family had not returned, but the airdrop had finally come! It was important that the relief workers drop the food bags in a good spot. They would make only one pass, in order to avoid the machine-gun fire of government troops hiding in the area.

The low-flying gray airplane, clearly marked with a large red cross circled in white, emerged from behind a row of trees. Stephen's mother frantically waved the scarf to attract their attention. "Here, here!" she cried. "Drop it here, away from the huts!"

And then it came, tumbling down, big white bags of sorghum, rice, cans of oil, bags of wheat, a box of malaria medicine. Some of the bags split open on impact, but no one cared. Everyone ran leaping and shouting into the field. Stephen's mother was crying with relief.

Banking sharply, rising higher and higher, the airplane disappeared.

Garang ran about giving orders. "Put all the wheat flour in one place. Then each family can come and take a bag!"

But no one listened. Everyone knew how to divide up the supplies. Mothers with small babies took the mosquito netting. In no time, several heavy sacks lay in each hut.

Stephen and Wol dragged the last one into the Majoks' tukel. Fifty pounds of rice. That would last forever! He couldn't understand the grim look on his mother's face. Why wasn't she laughing?

"Now we won't starve, Mama," Stephen said, dusting off his hands in satisfaction. "It doesn't matter if that sorghum in the field grows or not."

"Nonsense," his mother said. "At some point, these bags will be empty. One day the United Nations will go away. And then what? Those relief planes won't keep this up forever."

Stephen didn't want to listen to words like that. To distract himself, he examined one of the small packages that the airplane had also dropped. The packs were shiny, with English letters printed on them. The boys had gathered handfuls of them. Stephen held the pack close and tried to read the label. " 'Ready Meal Pak,' " Stephen said slowly. " 'Just add H2O.' "

"What does that mean?" Wol asked.

"I don't know." Stephen tore open the bag. Dry, powdery brown dust fell onto the dirt floor.

He licked his finger and tasted some. "Pfew. It's terrible. Maybe it's a kind of coffee."

"Maybe it's cow dung," said Wol, teasing.

Stephen threw the empty wrapper at him. "It's not dung. But probably we should burn it. It tastes very bad."

"So, Auntie Deborah," said Wol, sitting next to Naomi and her mother. "We should make some kind of plan."

"Plan? For what?" asked Stephen, dusting the powder off his hands.

"Don't be foolish, Stephen. Why don't you think for once? Now that a food drop has come, soldiers will raid us," Naomi said harshly. "We are nearly starving, so we beg for food. But when it comes, who knows what will happen. Don't you remember the last time?"

Of course he remembered, even though he tried not to. Tears suddenly filled his eyes. He felt hopeless, unable to control anything. Stephen went and lay down on his sleeping mat. He stared at the straw-and-mud wall inches from his face. Every time something good happened in the village, disaster came along afterward.

Naomi was right about the soldiers. They had raided the village just a few days after the last food drop. They stole the bags of grain and some cows, including one of the Majoks'. Their biggest white one. The strong and healthy one. It wasn't that Stephen had forgotten; he just didn't want to think about it.

The boys and Naomi had hidden in an earthen tunnel in the brush, which their mothers had dug to hide the children and whatever food they could during raids. After the soldiers finally left, Stephen and the others found some cows gone and several huts burned to the ground.

But that was months and months ago. And Stephen had tried hard to go on as though nothing were wrong. What else could they do? No one came to help. Stephen brought his knees up close to his chest and rocked himself a little bit.

"You're right, Wol," his mother said. "We need a plan. How long can I keep hiding you all in tunnels like little animals? You must go to school. This is the modern age. It's the only way we will survive, if you can go to school and study. You can't grow up knowing only how to steal cows from the next village."

No one spoke. Stephen waited breathlessly to hear what his mother would say next.

"Someday, the Americans will come and stop this terrible war. But who knows when that will be? We can't wait for that. We'll take our cows and leave for the border, Wol," she said. "In the refugee camps, there are schools."

Leave the village? But which way would they go? Their village was very isolated. People in larger villages had left the area several years ago. There were no roads that Stephen knew of, only dusty cattle paths to follow. And those paths mostly led to water holes or streams that were now dried up.

There was one large path, though, that led north to the River of Gazelles. Stephen had taken the cows there once to bathe them. And where did the small paths go? Stephen didn't know. He wasn't sure his mother knew, either.

"When would we leave, Mama?" Naomi asked.

"I don't know yet. I have to think about it. Now, don't tell anyone. Do you hear me?"

Stephen rolled over to stare at her. "Why not?"

"Because I think there are informers here. In this village with us. People who have many cows still.

Those people will tell something like this to soldiers to keep their own cows safe. Especially someone who might be angry at the others."

And that was the worst thing she had ever said. Stephen was sure she meant that Garang was an informer.

Six

But the next morning, the sun rose as usual. Nothing's going to happen, Stephen told himself as he went to fetch the cows. Everyone's worrying for nothing.

When they reached the pasture area, the boys lined up to throw their spears. Wol drew a line in the dirt so they would be even at the start. Stephen went first and threw his in a high arc, and perhaps the wind caught it, because it landed well into the tangled brush at the edge of the dry pasture. It was his farthest throw ever.

"Oh, wow!" he teased. "Look at that. You can't beat me, either of you! I may be the youngest, but I'm the strongest."

"And you'll never find your spear again in that mess of bushes!" Deng shouted after him as Stephen ran to search for his spear.

Stephen was annoyed when he couldn't find it.

"More to the left," Wol called. "You're not looking in the right spot."

Suddenly, for no particular reason, as Stephen stood there, prying apart the branches of bushes, he felt anxious and afraid. His mother's fear had just sunk down deep inside him. Last night he'd heard her talking about leaving, but it was only now that he understood all of what she had meant. He felt so afraid that he wasn't sure he could feel his own body, as if he were in his own dream, as though this had already happened once before.

But now he saw it. There was his spear. Just as Wol had said, farther to the left. And his life left its dreamy state and shifted back into everydayness again. He seized the spear and ran to his friends, pushing his fear aside.

"Let's stop this. It's too hot to throw spears, anyhow," said Wol. "Let's lie down in the shade."

"Fine with me," said Deng.

Stephen collapsed and lay still, his eyes closed.

"Hey," said Wol. "Where did your family members go when they went for the food drop, Deng?"

"I don't know. Maybe they went to Ethiopia," Deng said. "Or maybe Juba, way to the south."

"Did they ever reach a camp?" Wol asked.

"How would I know?"

"Deng, you're such an idiot," Wol said angrily.

"I'm not an idiot," Deng said. "I'm smarter than you."

"If you were smarter than me, you'd have worked out a plan."

"I will. Give me time, that's all." He rolled over on his back and shut his eyes. Wol tossed bits of twigs at him in disgust.

Stephen wished Wol hadn't brought up the subject of plans. "Hey, Wol. Do you think we'll ever really have to leave here?" he asked, looking up at the brilliant blue sky. Flies buzzed in the hot, dry grass beside his ears. He was sure they wouldn't leave. This was his place on earth.

"I don't know, Stephen. Yes. We will leave. I wish we knew where Deng's family went. Deng, you know what's wrong with you? You want to know why you don't know anything? It's because you are too lazy to remember. Remembering is too much work," grumbled Wol irritably.

"Of course I remember things! I'm trying to, anyway. I know they used to talk about going to a camp someplace," Deng said. "I think it was in Ethiopia."

"Oh, sure. That's a big help," Wol replied. "You know you're just guessing."

"Stop it, you two!" Stephen shouted. "Be quiet!"

He couldn't stand listening to them. He sat up, uncorked his goatskin bag, and took a long drink of water. He could feel the coolness trickle all the way down his throat into his stomach. Sometimes a drink of water was the only way he could calm himself.

Wol sat up and took a long drink, too.

"Hey, look! My mother's coming!" Wol exclaimed as he put the stopper back in the bag.

Dressed in a long yellow skirt and T-shirt and a head scarf wrapped turban-style over her hair, Wol's mother, Mary, hurried across the pasture.

"Boys, come on!" she called, waving to them. "Bring the cows. Come home, quick!"

Uneasily, the boys rounded up the cows into a tight group, tapping them on their bony rumps with long sticks to get them moving toward the village. They jogged after them, despite the heat.

In their tukel, Stephen's mother was gathering his few belongings and beginning to stow them in the backpack the teacher had given him. The letters "UN" had once been written on it in white. She took off one of her necklaces and slipped the strand of coral beads around his neck.

"What are you doing?" Stephen asked, staring down at his chest, looking closely at the sunset-colored beads.

"For luck. And here. Take these shoes," she said, plopping two large shoes without laces in front of his bare feet. "Put them on!"

Naomi stood by, watching, her arms wrapped around her stomach as though she were hugging herself.

"No, Mama! I can't wear these. They'll fall off. Anyway, my pencil was in them and now it's missing. Where's my pencil?"

"Take the shoes!" she shouted at him in exasperation. "Hurry!"

"But, why? What's happening?" Stephen asked, near tears.

Naomi answered. "I went to the well. And there was an explosion. I heard a bomb. The soldiers are coming here."

"Take this goatskin. Go refill it."

His mother handed him the bag stoppered with a small cork.

"Wait a minute. I want to take my pencil with me. Where did it go? Naomi, help me look. Please?"

He pawed frantically through the small pile of belongings his mother had gathered, looking for the pencil, one of his prized possessions. Before the schoolteacher left last year, he gave each pupil a pencil. Stephen's was blue, with silver stars. Wol and Deng promptly lost theirs, but he had kept his in one of the big shoes. From time to time, he took it out and day-dreamed about how one day he would be a teacher himself.

"I said go for water. Now!" his mother urged. Then she turned her back on him and crouched by the fire, her hands over her face, and began sobbing.

"I found it. Here's your pencil, Stephen," Naomi said, putting it in his pack.

Stephen gave her a smile. Then he kicked off the big shoes and ran to the well.

If he had to leave with the other boys, he would be a man now, wouldn't he, as Wol almost was? Where would they go? Just into the trees nearby? Was the forest far enough to wait out the attack of the northern government soldiers? And his mother and sister would wait here, guarding the cows, the cotton crop they sold for lentils, rice, beans, and tea? The well, and its precious water? With Naomi in the tunnel?

The little boy who tended the cow at the well wasn't there. Neither was the cow. So Stephen drew on the thin rope that dangled into the deep well and pulled violently. And then he stopped. He heard it, too. A boom, far away, like thunder. But it wasn't thunder. It didn't have the rattly, raggedy sound of thunder at all.

It was deep and short and even, a sound made by a machine, not by nature.

Hurriedly he poured the water from the bucket into the narrow neck of the goatskin water bag, spilling some on the ground at his feet. His hands were shaking so that he couldn't help spilling it. He had hardly got the stopper back in before he turned and ran back to his tukel.

"I heard explosions, too, Mama," he said. "Just now."

"Yes, yes. So did I."

Quickly she washed his hands and wiped them with a small cloth. She washed the dirt off his face and placed the pack on his back. She took his face in her hands. "They'll come and try to take you to train as a soldier. So you boys, you, Deng, and Wol, will hide. In the forest. No, go farther. Go farther away than that. And wait till they've gone. They won't stay here long. You'll be home soon, maybe even by tomorrow. And then everything will be fine, Stephen. Just like it was before. Naomi will hide food in the tunnels, and take some goats and chickens. We have to save as much food as we can."

"Shouldn't Naomi come with us and leave the animals?" he asked. "She can hide with us. Won't that be safer?"

"No. Naomi has to guard the goats and chickens."

Already Naomi was gathering up food sacks. She caught a hen and bound its legs with string and laid it on the ground beside the grain.

"All right, now," his mother said. "Go. Put your shoes on and go. Everything will be all right."

Stephen hugged his mother and then Naomi. Then he ran.

Seven

At the edge of the pasture, Deng and Wol met Stephen.

"Just a minute," he said, gasping, glad of the opportunity to remove the big shoes and stuff them into his pack, and to duck his head and wipe away his tears.

"Maybe this will be fun," Wol said, clapping him on the back to encourage him. "The soldiers will be gone soon. Don't worry."

"Yeah. We can pretend to be white people on safari on the plains of Africa," Deng said. "In Kenya. Lion hunters. Elephant hunters. Rich people in Jeeps!"

"They're called tourists. They aren't real hunters," Wol said. "But you know what they have that would be good? Binoculars."

He put his cupped hands to his eyes, pretending to scan the horizon. "You can see for miles with those. You can see everything."

"No. I've changed my mind. We shouldn't be safari guys," Deng said. "We should be aid workers. Then we could eat all day long. Sorghum porridge with sweet tea? Beans? Coca-Cola?"

Stephen smiled. He knew they were kidding around with him because they could see how frightened he was. He'd be all right with his friends, he told himself. Anyway, they could all go home tomorrow. Hadn't his mother said so?

The boys set out across the fields, hurrying to reach the trees and brush. It was a fine day, not as hot as yesterday, fortunately, and locusts whirred in between the stalks. The grass smelled fresh and dry, a little like bread cooking.

Perhaps grass stalks were a bit like wheat, Stephen thought. He had never considered that before. He plucked one of the stiff, dry stalks and chewed on it for a few minutes as he hurried after the other two. What would it be like to eat grass the way cows did?

Goats could eat anything. He wondered how Naomi was doing in the tunnel with the animals. The goats would nibble her dress and flip-flops. It wouldn't be fun at all to spend the night in the tunnel. Goats were so restless and pushy.

The boys started through the scrubby forest, which here was mostly dense brush interspersed with acacia trees. Sharp thorns and branches scratched their legs, and Wol used his spear to beat the bushes in front of him because he was afraid of stepping on snakes.

"That's far enough. This is silly. How can an army catch us in here?" asked Deng after a few minutes. "They would be wasting their time. Let's stop and rest. Maybe it's best not to go too far. That way we can still hear if there's an attack at home."

Out of breath already, the boys stopped and sat down. Months of not having quite enough to eat made them tire quickly. Stephen slipped the water bag off his shoulder, and they each took a small sip.

As they sat together quietly, the enormity of army soldiers attacking their small, defenseless village of huts sank in. Each boy thought of the terrible things that might happen to his family, the cows, the well.

"Your mother should have let Naomi come with us. They kidnap girls, I heard," said Wol.

"No they don't. Girls can't fight for them," scoffed Stephen angrily. He couldn't bear to think about that.

"They don't take them to fight. They sell them as slaves," Deng said. "Slave dealers take them north to work for the Arabs."

Stephen's eyes widened. "No they don't."

"Yes they do!" cried Deng, kicking him. "Everyone knows that. People in the North buy them to work on farms and in rich people's houses."

"Stop kicking me. That hurt, Deng."

"Sorry." Deng covered his face with his hands, just the way Stephen's mother had.

Was that why his mother had yelled, he wondered, because she was so worried, knowing that Naomi might be kidnapped? At the time, he had been thinking only of himself, looking frantically for his pencil. His mother had taught him to think of himself first. That wasn't wrong. After all, *he* was the boy. He would be in charge of their household someday.

"How do we know if we're heading in the right direction?" Wol asked.

"Why are you asking that? What is the right direction?" asked Stephen. "We don't know where the soldiers are."

"What kind of soldiers are they, do you think?" asked Deng.

"Government ones. From the North," Stephen said without raising his head.

"How do you know? They could be other tribespeople coming to steal grain and cattle," Wol said, arguing with him now. "Or even some friends of Garang. You know he's angry with us."

"Come off it, Wol. He can't be mean enough to betray his own village," Deng said.

"Yeah. And his friends wouldn't have guns. They wouldn't have big weapons like that. I heard the explosions myself," Stephen said. "Only the North has bombs that large."

"Okay. Okay. Stop arguing. Look, never mind who they are. It doesn't matter," said Wol. "We're just hiding for now. That's all."

They fell silent. Stephen wondered if Garang's friends would come looking for them in particular. But was Peter really a traitor? It was impossible to know.

"My mother said we can go home again tomorrow," Stephen said.

"Really? My mother said we should never go back. Anyway, what did you bring with you?" Deng asked. "Any food?"

The boys opened their backpacks and examined what each of them had brought. Deng had brought a Bible because he was Christian, like many southern Sudanese. Wol and Stephen held traditional, tribal beliefs. The schoolteacher had been Christian, though, so they knew about the Bible. A little.

Besides his shoes, Stephen had his pencil, his geography book, two flat breads, an extra shirt, and a long piece of cloth his mother used as a headdress sometimes. Wol had two dried figs, some cold beans, and a few pieces of caramel candy. Deng had handfuls of rice wrapped in a cloth.

Looking at all the food spread out on their packs

made their stomachs growl. They decided to eat. Convinced they would go back home soon, they ate nearly everything but the uncooked rice, saving some bread and candy for later on. Then they lay back on their packs, talking quietly and waiting.

The afternoon wore slowly on, until the sun began to sink through the trees in the west, growing fatter and more deeply orange as it went down. All day, the sun had shone almost directly overhead. Sudan was so near the equator that the boys had to wait until the sun started to set to be sure in which direction they were headed.

"So, by looking at the sun now," said Stephen, "I think we were headed southeast."

"If we leave the area, is that a good way to go?" asked Deng.

"I don't know. Maybe we should go to Kenya," Wol said. "Where is Kenya? You tell us, Stephen. You got a hundred in geography last year."

"Okay." Stephen opened his geography book. "I—"

Then they heard distant gunfire. The rattle of machine guns echoed around them. The sound seemed to bounce off the tree trunks. The boys crouched together, frozen, straining to hear what was happening, but at the same time not wanting to hear at all. They heard louder bursts of grenades. Stephen shoved his fist in his mouth to stop his sobs. Deng covered his ears and slowly rocked back and forth. Wol hugged his pack tightly to his chest.

The noise seemed to last forever, rattling and popping. So many bullets had to be flying. But when the shooting stopped, Stephen noticed that the sun was still a flat red disk through the trees, casting a red glow on everything. It didn't seem to have moved at all.

Eight

That night was cold, as it always was in the savanna after a clear, cloudless day. And none of them could sleep. They huddled together for warmth under the cloth that Stephen had brought.

After a long and terrible night, silent, without even the calls of animals, the boys went back to the village early, before the sun came up. No one spoke on the way. Across the pasture, they saw the smoking remains of the grass huts, most of them now burned to the ground. The pen for the goats had been trampled. They didn't hear the cluck of hens, chasing insects for breakfast.

The boys entered the village slowly. They stood still, watching the strands of smoke rise, swaying skyward in slow-dancing soft loops of pale gray. They stood for a long time, waiting and listening, not feeling. But still there was no sound, not of voices or of cattle or of chickens. There was only the smell of smoke.

As they listened, they noticed the gentle cracklings of dying embers, the soft hisses as beads of moisture bubbled and escaped from bundles of burned grass that had collapsed into heaps of ash. But they knew they heard these things only because it was so absolutely quiet, without even the chirps of birds, as though nature itself had fled.

Stephen went to the well with its wall of mud-baked bricks and peered in. The rope for the well had been cut and taken away. Then he turned and looked from hut to hut. Most of the tukels were burned to the ground; others stood empty, including Peter Garang's. Inside the ones still standing, grain baskets were knocked over, beans spilled across the dirt floor. And the large bags of grain and the goats, cows, and chickens were all gone.

Stephen's tukel was one of those not burned. He walked toward it.

"Mama? Mama, it's me!" he called. He was almost hoping there would be no answer, for how could he ever take care of her if she was wounded and alive?

He ducked his head and entered and saw immediately that his mother was there, dead. Keeping his eyes averted, he quickly covered her with a straw mat. Then he whirled around. Naomi—where was she? She couldn't still be in the tunnel. Why wasn't she here? Maybe she'd been tied up with the well rope and led away, he thought as he stood by the smashed shards of wood that had once been their low eating table. He had to go search the tunnel for her, but he was afraid to. After what he had just seen, he was afraid of everything. So he stood there, not moving at all except for the trembling of his knees.

Why didn't Naomi come? Where was she? He was so angry with her for not being there!

He felt as though he were watching himself from someplace outside his body. He didn't cry. He didn't move. He only stood and saw himself, a small boy dressed in a T-shirt and tan shorts.

Once the teacher had brought a black-and-white television set to school and connected it to his kerosene-run generator. The kids had watched some people on the screen talking about boiling water to clean it and about HIV illness. Then they got to watch a soccer game. The players had colorful uniforms and ran about on bright green grass in a large stadium. After that, an aid worker took the television away in a white Jeep. Stephen was watching himself now the same way he had watched the athletes on television that time.

Finally he stooped and gathered some beans by the handful, dropping them into his pack. But now what? He should take some things, he thought. But he found again that he couldn't move. He simply stared at all their shattered belongings before him, not knowing what to do.

Stephen pulled the big, useless shoes out of his pack and put in a metal spoon, the little pocketknife, his math book, and his English book. He scooped up some rice and dumped it in the bottom of the pack with the beans.

He was very careful not to look at his mother. But as he was leaving, he went back. Still not looking, he lifted the straw mat and slipped the last string of coral beads off her neck and pushed it hurriedly into his pack. One day he would wear it.

His mother was gone, but he would always honor her. She would always be a part of his life. If people didn't treat him well in this world, she would send an illness for him. And that illness would bring him back to her and make them close again. That was how it went. Children could be fetched from this world.

He felt the pressure of tears along the ridge of his cheekbones and behind his eyes. But the tears never reached his eyes. They stayed invisible, underground, like the well water the boys couldn't reach. Instead, he simply screamed, his eyes closed, his face upraised. One long, loud roar of pain like that of a wounded animal, a lioness whose cub has died. And when that sound stopped coming from him, when his throat was raw and sore, he stood in silence and heard nothing but his own breathing, raspy and slow.

Stephen sat at the edge of the village and waited for his friends. He knew they would come there to find him. But he didn't dare go looking for them because he couldn't face what he would probably find. He couldn't begin to think of searching the tunnel without them, so he waited at the field, where they always waited for one another. When he closed his eyes, he saw afterimages of how the fire from the burning huts had died down, leaving thick circles of glowing sparks. He sat there for hours.

Now it was nearly night. His friends would look for him in his hut and then come here. So he waited.

The boys came alone, without any family members. He didn't know how to ask what they had found, so he said nothing.

"Where's Naomi?" Wol asked.

He didn't answer. Later Wol went to check the tunnel. He came back alone. There was nothing to say. Somehow, they slept.

Nine

Three days passed before any of them began talking again. For those three days, the boys pushed slowly and mindlessly through the brush and forest, eating handfuls of dry beans and rice from their bundles from time to time, before they emerged again into more grasslands dotted with thorny acacia trees.

For another long day, they crossed a huge expanse of dry grass under the burning sun, walking slowly south. Their drinking water was now gone. Flies pestered them, the way they usually did the cows, clustering around the boys' eyes in search of traces of moisture. It was hot, well over one hundred degrees.

Finally, Deng stopped walking. He swayed a little on his feet. Then he sat down and began to cry. Wol knelt beside him and licked the tears off his cheeks before the sun could dry them. He waved Stephen over. Stephen licked the tears, too, for a moment.

The slight moisture and saltiness only made him wilder with thirst. It was impossible to think of anything else, not his mother or sister or anything. Only thirst. It battered about inside him like a desperate, scrabbling animal.

Here in the grasslands, there were barely any green leaves to suck on. The boys chewed twigs for slight, quickly forgotten drops of moisture. Or when there were no twigs, they sucked on stones.

Now they were so drained they simply sat. A slight breeze rippled the dry tawny grasses, which made a soft scratching sound as they rubbed together.

Stephen sniffed. He sniffed again. Very faintly, he thought he smelled the scent of fire. Something had burned. Was it their village he could smell? Had they walked in a complete circle? Had they walked all the way back home?

Hope leaped in his chest. If they followed the smell, they would find a village, burned like theirs probably, but perhaps with grains of food, or a well, or even people, grownups, who would help them.

"Come on," he said, too weak even to explain to the others. "Come on, Deng. Just a little farther. There's a village. I'm sure of it."

In ten minutes' walking they came to a well-trampled dirt track, and they followed it, their hopefulness renewing their energy. They walked slowly. In the late afternoon full of the sloping golden rays from the sun, they saw the back of a cow standing in the grass, the thrust of its rear pelvic bones, the tips of its horns. Three young boys rose to their feet and came out of the grass and stared at them.

"Hello! Did the soldiers come here? Was your village burned?" Wol asked in Dinka, the common language of the hundreds of different southern tribes.

"Salaam aleekam," the boys murmured nervously in Arabic. Peace be with you.

"We're not northern soldiers. Don't be afraid of us. Your village?" asked Stephen in Dinka. "Is it burned?"

One boy said, "Yesterday."

"Did you see who did it? Were they government soldiers?" asked Deng. "Is that why you thought we were Muslims?"

They shrugged. Two of the boys looked like brothers, about seven and eight. The other boy was tall, the tallest and thinnest of all of them. His teeth pressed forward so that he couldn't quite close his lips. Somehow his teeth frightened Stephen. They reminded him of a mask.

"Don't you know who came?" Deng asked again.

"Stop it, Deng, it doesn't matter. Probably the same soldiers who burned our village," Wol said.

"Oh. Hey! Does that cow of yours give milk?" Deng asked, pointing.

"A little."

Quickly, Deng, Wol, and Stephen squatted by the cow's bony flank while the oldest boy tried to pull milk from her into their open mouths. But she gave each of them only a few swallows. Still, Stephen felt rejuvenated. He sat back on his heels and grinned at his friends. Smiling felt funny.

"We hid here in the tall grass when the soldiers came. We made the cow lie down," the littlest one said to Stephen.

"We were afraid she would make noise, but if we let her go, they might capture her. Anyway, they didn't find us," said his older brother proudly.

Stephen nodded. He wanted to know if they could go into their village and search for food there, but he knew that it would be terrible to do that, and so he couldn't ask. Not right away.

"We're going to Kenya," he said instead. "There is a refugee camp there, run by the United Nations. And they have schools at that camp."

"We are?" Wol asked. "When did we decide?"

"You're crazy, Stephen. Kenya is much too far."

Deng said. "Who has a Jeep? We can't make it on foot."

"Of course we can. You're lazy, both of you," he said. "I bet these little boys aren't as lazy as you."

Deng frowned and hit the cow on the side with his stick. The cow moved away.

"Hey!" said the tall one. "Don't. We saved this cow from the soldiers, but not so you could hit her."

He pushed Deng backward, and Deng sat down hard in the dusty track. The little boys laughed at him. Wol stood beside Deng and pulled him to his feet again.

"You should come with us. We need food and water if we're going to travel all that way to the camp," Wol said to the tall boy. "What's your name?"

"Jairo. And he is Henry, and the littlest one is Simon."

"Where's your well?" Stephen asked. "We're so thirsty."

Jairo frowned. "The soldiers threw a dead goat into it. We checked already."

"I don't care about the goat," said Deng. "We must have water."

"Okay. Come on," Jairo said. "But Simon and Henry can wait here. It's not good for them to see what happened."

Wol had already started off.

"I'll stay with them," Deng said. "But, Stephen, be sure to bring me plenty of water."

Stephen knew that Deng was afraid.

As they neared the circle of burned huts, the smell of fire grew much stronger. Stephen stooped to examine the ashes, patting and sifting through them, looking for live coals to start a fire. He burned his fingers picking up glowing bits of the straw mixed with mud that the tukels had been made of. He heaped the coals in a pile, blowing gently to make them burn brighter. Gradually he added a few twigs, then a few more, then a stick or two. And soon he had a small, crackling fire.

The well stood in the circle of shade from two trees. Wol and Jairo returned with a bucket of water.

"We have to boil it first," Stephen said, dusting off his hands. "Because of the goat."

The schoolteacher had told them always to boil water or they could catch cholera. It had been on that television they'd seen, too.

"What? Oh. No. I can't wait for that."

Wol tipped the bucket to his lips and took a huge swallow. He groaned with relief as he let the water trickle down his parched throat. "Ahhh. That feels wonderful!"

"Stop it, Wol. It will make you sick." Stephen took hold of the bucket. "Help me find more wood to burn so we can boil the water."

"You aren't the boss of everyone," Wol said, trying to grab the bucket back. He ended up knocking it to the ground. The water spilled onto the packed dirt.

Stephen, dizzy now, closed his eyes with exhaustion.

"You shouldn't argue like that. Look how tired he is. I'll get some more water, and I know where there is some charcoal to keep the fire going," Jairo said.

Ten

They stayed near the village, by the dirt track, and slept in the grass beside the cow for three nights. On the third morning, the boys sat up, stiff and cold from sleeping on the ground. Each day, they argued for hours about what to do.

"I think we should forget about the refugee camps. We should join the rebel side," Wol said. "The soldiers will feed us and train us."

"Rebels?" asked Jairo. "Which group? I'm fifteen, old enough to fight. But we have to be careful. What if we join a gang of outlaws by mistake?"

"Wol doesn't know where the rebels are. You're showing off, Wol," said Deng.

"We're all still children. We should find a refugee camp so we can go to school," Stephen said. He knew that was what his mother had wanted. "There's a school in the camp in Kenya. I'm sure of it. Then we will be educated when the war is over."

"When the war is over," Wol echoed in disgust. "We'll be one hundred by then."

"No we won't," Stephen said stubbornly.

"I don't think we should go to Kenya," Jairo said. "How will we get across the border? I bet there are lots of northern soldiers there, just waiting to capture kids like us. We should go to the Central African Republic. That's where Dinka can go safely. The Nuer tribe goes to Kenya."

"Who made those rules?" Wol asked. "We can go wherever we want."

"Everybody, hush!" Deng shouted suddenly, his eyes wide with fear. "Listen!"

They heard the roar of plane engines.

"Get down! Stay in the tall grass," Wol shouted. "Lie down flat on your stomachs."

The sound of the planes came closer and closer.

"What if they see us?" Simon asked. "What will they do?"

"Quiet," Wol ordered. "Get down."

"Our cow!" Henry shouted, kneeling up to look for her.

"Let her go! Don't move!" Stephen hissed, pulling Henry down next to him.

The boys lay in the tall grass as the northern government planes approached, flying low over the grasslands, following the narrow dirt track that led past the ruined village. One plane flew directly above the boys, casting a swift-moving shadow over them like the shadow of a big, dark bird. As the plane flew past, Stephen glanced cautiously up and saw that the side door was open. Three soldiers were crouched there, and one had a machine gun ready. He saw the soldiers point at the cow, which by now had wandered away from the children down the track.

The machine gun burst into action, spraying bullets, and the cow fell to the ground.

Henry cried out, but Stephen pulled him close and covered his mouth with his hand.

"Shut up," he whispered to the little boy. "Do you want to get us killed? Now, lie still."

A second plane came and passed directly over the burned village. The roar of the engines faded into the distance. And then there was silence. Slowly, the boys got to their feet.

"What should we do now?" Wol asked.

"We can't stay here," Jairo said.

"We'll have to walk at night," Deng said. "Or those planes might see us."

"But our cow!" Simon said. And because he started crying, Henry cried, too.

All the boys were upset. Cows were sacred animals that prolonged life. Cows gave them everything they needed to survive in the grasslands. They had been taught that since they were born.

But they couldn't stay near the ruined village any longer. At night, they were calling out with bad dreams, nightmares. Now they would have to rest during the day and walk at night, relying on moonlight and starlight, in order to hide from the low-flying planes.

"So," Stephen said, "where does this track go? Does it lead to a road? Is that why the plane was following it?"

"Yes," Jairo answered. "It goes to a dirt road eventually. There even used to be a bus, years ago. And if you travel east, maybe for a day or two walking, I think there is a river. Several years ago there was. Maybe it's dried up now from the drought. I don't know."

"Hey! A river? The White Nile?" Stephen asked, his eyes wide.

"No," said Jairo. "Just a very small river."

"Oh."

Stephen was disappointed. He had always dreamed of sailing north on that long, long river, past the ancient temples, through the cataracts, the Nubian desert—maybe all the way to Cairo, thousands of miles to the north. Or maybe he would sail south and reach the Nile source, near Lake Victoria, east of the Mountains of the Moon. That had a beautiful sound.

Maybe he would travel east to the Red Sea someday. Or to the Indian Ocean and the islands that lined Africa's east coast, with their palm trees and sea breezes. His teacher had been to one of those islands and had told him.

"Anyway, one day, if we keep walking east, we *will* cross the Nile," Stephen said stubbornly. "And after that, there is Ethiopia and Kenya. Here, I'll show you. Look, everyone."

He opened his backpack and took out the geography book. "Lower Sudan. There is the White Nile. There is Ethiopia."

"Why is this part so dark brown?" Jairo asked.

"That's Kenya. Those brown patches are its tall mountains. The map shows them in brown. Three miles high, the mountains are. With snow on top. See the white spots?"

"Snow?" asked Simon, and all the boys laughed.

"Maybe Santa Claus lives there," Deng said.

"Who?" asked Henry.

"He's a guy who brings toys to kids in England. Our teacher told us about him. He comes when it snows."

"How does snow taste?" Jairo asked.

"Cold, dummy," Wol answered.

"Is it sweet, like milk with sugar?" Simon asked.

"I think it tastes like rain," Deng said. "It comes from clouds. And it sticks to mountaintops."

"Never mind that. Okay, Stephen. Just how far is Kenya?" Jairo asked.

Stephen measured what he thought might be the distance with a stalk of grass. Then he laid the length of grass against the mileage key. "About four hundred miles," he muttered, closing the book.

"You're crazy!" Jairo shouted at him. "You know that? You're a dreamer. A crazy person. We're children. Orphans now, all six of us. How can we walk so far? When we leave the village, who knows what it will be like. Maybe we'll be eaten by lions. Or attacked by robbers and soldiers."

"No we won't," said Wol, getting to his feet and putting on his pack. "It won't be like that at all. We got here, didn't we? We'll be all right. Let's just continue south for now."

Wol picked up Stephen's goatskin water bag and three plastic soda bottles that they had found near the well. "Come on, help me fill these," he said to Jairo. "And stop scaring everyone, will you?"

From the ruined huts, Deng and Stephen gathered several cups of rice. They carried them back to the little boys.

When the sun began to set, the group packed up their few belongings.

"It's time to go," Stephen said, squatting down beside Simon and Henry.

They didn't move.

"Yeah," said Jairo. "Come on."

"Get up!" said Wol.

Stephen nodded to his friends to start walking. But the little boys stayed as still as tree stumps.

"It's too bad you aren't coming, because every morning, we will have school," Stephen said loudly. "You won't need a pencil. It will be dirt school. I can draw the letters in the dirt. English letters. We will all learn to read English. I brought my English book with me. You'll see. We'll be fine, I promise you. And soon you'll be able to write all the letters for yourself, whenever you want. Anyway, we should get started now. It's not likely the planes will come here again today."

He, Wol, Jairo, and Deng were walking farther and farther away. Finally Simon and Henry ran after them. They had no choice.

Eleven

They walked for three nights along the narrow dirt track, but there was no sign of the road Jairo had promised. Maybe they had walked too slowly. In the darkness, it was impossible to have any sense of how far they'd gone.

And once more they grew hungry and thirsty. The days were bright and hot, making it hard to sleep. As they rested, Stephen drew one letter per day in the dirt: A, B, C. In English. He taught them the sounds for each one.

As they walked at night, swarms of mosquitoes hovered around them in thick clouds, clogging their noses, their eyes and ears. In desperation, they covered their arms and faces with dust to prevent the mosquitoes from biting.

"With all these mosquitoes," Jairo said, "I'm sure we're nearing that river I was thinking of."

The thought of a river, of bathing in cool water, made them walk a little faster. They heard the high-pitched squeak of bats diving for insects and the harsh, barking cough of lions, as though they had choked on something and were trying to cough it up. An hour passed. Then another. There was no river.

Stephen felt cold and lonely, walking at night. It was hard to see the ground, and they all stumbled often, tripping over sticks, stepping into holes, and twisting their ankles. All the time, he wished for his mother, and he was sure that the others did, too. But most of the villagers were dead, the huts burned, the cows stolen. He wiped the tears from his cheeks.

To keep himself going, he tried to make friends with the stars that hung so brightly over the savanna, and began giving them names. Peeker. Little John. Bright Eyes. The north star he knew. It was the star that never moved. They kept that at their backs all night long.

To cheer themselves up, they sang—songs about the sun coming up, the rainy season, pounding grain for bread, songs about beautiful girls, hunting, and cattle.

Toward sunup on the third day, they stopped, completely exhausted. Stephen stared overhead at the sky. Star after star grew tiny and faded as the dawn turned the sky from black to pale gray to pink.

"We must have walked right past that road in the

dark, Jairo," Deng suggested. "Maybe it was covered over by sand from a windstorm."

"How could we miss a road?" Jairo countered.

Deng shrugged. He sat down.

Stephen sat, too. His eyes closed while he rested with his head on his drawn-up knees. He dozed off. He didn't care if a haboob, a violent storm of wind and sand, came. He wanted to be whirled into the air in a cloud of blowing dust. Maybe he could be dropped down someplace far, far away—a cold, snowy Santa Claus place full of shiny cars, televisions, relief workers, and smooth roads. With big, green soccer fields to play ball on.

And then that dream blew away and he dreamed of a fierce man who said he was his father, a soldier, and now he was urging them on, telling them they were men, not boys. And they should fight back. Retaliate. Someday they would be soldiers for the South, and they would defeat the northern side. But Stephen didn't want to be a soldier, shooting cows, killing children's mothers, stealing food. What kind of life was that? He wanted to be a teacher.

He woke up again, shaking his head to free himself of drowsiness. He was a dreamer: Jairo was right about that.

While the others slept, Stephen took his geography

book out of his pack. It was in English, hard to read. He took his stick and wrote in the dust: "Sudan is a very ancient country." He read the first words aloud: "Sudan is a very . . ." But the last two words he didn't know. "An . . . ankent . . ." Oh, well.

He wrote the letter "A" in the dust. Two days ago, that had been their letter. The next day, "B." Today their letter was "C." "C" had two sounds.

Anxiously, Stephen looked at the map in his book. They were headed toward an area where there were rivers. At least, he hoped so. On his map, it said "the Sudd," the giant swamp where the White Nile broke into a hundred shifting channels. There would be plenty of water to drink there.

But probably they had walked very slowly, more slowly than he had expected. Maybe they covered five miles per night. There was no way to know in the darkness. There was nothing to see. They were walking through a vast wasteland. The only real movement came from the dark-winged vultures circling overhead on the rising hot air. It seemed to Stephen that there were no people left in the whole world but them. And the truth was that he had no idea where they were.

"Look, everyone. 'A, B, C,' " he said loudly. "You see? And letter 'C' has two sounds, *cuh* and *sss*. Tomorrow's letter is 'D.' "

The boys sat up, but no one was interested. They stared at nothing. The flattened goatskin bag lay beside them. The empty soda bottles lay tipped on their sides. Henry unscrewed a cap and tried to drain an invisible drop of water into his parched throat. He threw the bottle in frustration and let it roll away.

"Pick up the bottle and put the cap back on," Deng muttered. "The bottle's useless without the cap."

"It's useless anyway," Jairo said, shielding Henry from Deng's anger.

"We can't lose the cap, Jairo," Stephen said. It seemed so ridiculous to be arguing over a little piece of plastic.

Simon scrambled to get the bottle. He took the cap from Henry and screwed it back on, and they all sat, thirsty, dusty, and exhausted. Stephen hugged him.

"Stephen," Simon said, "I don't want to chew leaves anymore. They taste so bitter. I'm not a giraffe."

"No, you'd need more spots," Stephen said, smiling.

"I don't have any spit left," said Simon.

Stephen nodded. His throat felt scratchy and dry, too. And his stomach ached with a terrible cramping sharpness. The handfuls of uncooked rice they'd been eating couldn't be good for them. But what could they do? They had to eat something. The only other choice was tree bark, twigs, or roots. And those tasted bitter and nasty. They had to have water. Never mind Kenya or wherever they were going.

Stephen got to his feet and picked up a soda bottle. He would go on ahead, along the track.

"I'm going to try to find the road and then come back for you. Rest under that tree there. Don't go anywhere else."

"Wait. I don't agree," said Wol. "We shouldn't split up under any conditions. You said so yourself fifty times."

Stephen looked at the two little boys, sprawled now on Jairo's lap, trying to sleep after their long night's walk.

"They're so tired. Besides, I won't go far."

"Shouldn't you wait? What about planes?" Deng asked.

"I'll hear them, won't I? I'll be careful," Stephen said.

Wol and Deng looked at Jairo to take their side. But he said nothing. So Stephen turned to leave.

"We'll wait for you here," Wol called.

Twelve

Stephen started walking. He walked for perhaps twenty minutes, then thirty, before he began to feel totally exhausted again. He trudged slowly up a small rise and started down the other side. Then he smelled something.

He stopped and sniffed the air carefully, like an animal. He smelled a kind of coolness. A cool dirt smell that could mean only one thing. The air had a pure, soft feel to it instead of its usual dryness.

Water. He sensed water.

He began to walk again. Yes, he smelled water! Definitely. But with it now were mixed other smells. And he stopped again, thinking, concentrating. Then he walked forward for a few more minutes.

He smelled something pungent, sharp. Something a little musty, like the smell of cow dung but much sharper and more frightening. He tried to ignore it. He had to get to the water.

There before him he saw not a river but a big muddy area. And in the center of the mud, surrounded by animal tracks of all kinds, was a broad, shallow pool of muddy water. Birds stood along its edge, dipping their beaks in for sips of water. Two of the birds were snowy white. Small egrets. Perhaps this was all that was left of the river that Jairo had remembered.

Stephen stopped, waited, thinking. If he could smell water, so could animals, whose senses were so much keener than people's.

Why weren't more animals here, drinking? Why only birds? Surely there must be a few gazelles still living nearby, even if he didn't see any. They must be thirsty, too.

He stepped carefully through the mud. Bones. The rib cage of an animal. A small gazelle or perhaps a large goat, the rib bones picked clean by vultures. A goat would mean that there was a village nearby, so it was probably a young gazelle.

And then he recognized the other smell.

Lion.

The smell seemed to come from everywhere. What if a group of lions was watching him from the tall grass right now? They were the same soft tan color, impossible to see. He looked again at the white rib bones. A gazelle had been surprised here, attacked by lions while drinking. If he was kneeling in the mud, filling the plastic bottle with water, the same could happen to him. One young boy would be easy prey for a bounding lioness. He shuddered with fear.

But he had to have water. Lions or no lions, he hurried forward, uncapped the soda bottle, and dipped it into the muddy pool. He drank, pouring the silty water down his dry throat in big gulps. He knew the water wasn't clean, but he was too thirsty to care. If he got sick, well, he would deal with that when it happened.

Several birds raised their wings and flapped away to watch him in safety. When the other birds noticed this, they, too, flocked together at a safe distance. He glanced at them and noticed that they stood facing in all directions, like lookouts. He smiled.

That was good, then. The birds were calm enough. They probably wouldn't be here at all if lions were nearby. He filled the bottle, hurried back to the track, and started up the small rise.

Now that he had the water and could think more clearly, Stephen was truly scared. What if the lions were stalking him, following him back to the others? When night fell, which would happen soon, they would all be easy prey for a lioness skilled in hunting.

He stooped to stuff the pockets of his shorts with small rocks from the track. Besides throwing rocks and shouting, he didn't know what else he could do to protect himself if he had to. Possibly climb a tree. But lions could climb, too.

Stephen took another sip of water. He tipped the bottle to his lips, not even minding the flat, silty, muddy taste or the grit on his teeth. The touch of the liquid soothed the back of his throat, clearing it of the dusty dryness and the harsh soreness of thirst. He took several more sips, and noticed that he breathed more easily when his throat was wet.

He went on again. A pocketful of stones to fight a lion? What good was that? He was a foolish child, afraid of everything. He wasn't a man at all, no matter what his dream father said. What a joke to pretend he was.

Stephen knew that the older villagers had hunted lions once, armed only with spears and a rifle. Now he wondered in awe at how they had done it and returned home alive.

———

The boys were elated when they saw the bottle of muddy water, and passed it around eagerly until it was empty moments later. They ignored the flat taste, the grit on their teeth.

"Let's go!" Jairo cried, jumping to his feet. "We have to get more. I'm still very, very thirsty."

"Wait!" said Stephen. "I have to explain something." He pulled some rocks from his pockets and dropped them at his feet. "There are lions there near the water hole."

"Did you see them?" Wol asked.

"No, but—"

"Then how do you know for sure?" Jairo asked. "You don't. Come on."

He pulled Simon and Henry to their feet and started off.

Stephen let his hands drop to his sides. He sighed deeply. "Their scent is everywhere. And there are no gazelles drinking. Only birds. I saw bones in the mud. Picked clean."

"Of course they're picked clean. Vultures do that in minutes," Wol said irritably.

"I heard that if a lion comes, you can stare at him without moving and he will eventually go away," Deng said. "My youngest uncle on my mother's side told me that."

"But what about hyenas? Where there are lions, there are hyenas." Wol argued. "You can't chase hyenas away no matter what you do. If you stare at them, they'll eat you anyway."

Why did Wol always argue? It was so tiring. Stephen didn't want to contradict the wisdom of Deng's uncle, who had gone to Khartoum to look for work three years ago and had never come back.

Then he heard himself asking something, too. "What if there are many lions all together? How can you stare at many of them when you have only one head?"

"Staring works better than a handful of rocks," argued Deng. "Getting hit by rocks will just enrage the lions. It won't hurt them. It won't even slow them down."

Stephen nodded. That made sense. But it seemed that every time they had to decide something, all they did was argue, the way kids always do. Whether to leave the cow, which way was Kenya. Now how to go about getting water.

And they should try somehow to boil this water before drinking it. Obviously, it was filthy and full of parasites. They had forgotten to bring coals from the fire they had made in Jairo's village. That was a big mistake. They didn't seem to think ahead at all. They just reacted to whatever desperate thought they had at the moment.

They could have carried some coals in a pan or tin. Perhaps it made sense to go back for that fire, Stephen thought. Fire would scare off the lions at night, too, and help get rid of mosquitoes. How had they made such a mistake?

Suddenly, Stephen felt hopeful. Yes. They needed fire right now, more than anything. They had to have both fire and water to survive day after day.

"We should return for some burning charcoal from Jairo's village," he said abruptly. "Even if it is three nights' walk. That's what we'll do."

"No, Stephen," Wol said, more gently than usual. "The charcoal embers will have gone out by now."

"Yeah," Deng added. "Besides, the soldiers could spot a fire from the air."

"Oh," said Stephen, feeling foolish. And then he burst into tears. He wanted his mother or his sister, Naomi, to take care of these things for him. Naomi was sixteen. How was he to know what was best?

Wol, who somehow had lost his shirt during the walk the night before and now wore only a pair of tattered, filthy shorts, put his arm around Stephen like a brother. And Stephen pressed his face against the warmth of Wol's skin for comfort. He wished that Wol and Naomi had been married, even for only a day.

"Come on, Stephen. Hey! You did a wonderful thing, finding water for us. But we can't stay here and let the others drink it all," said Deng.

They set off down the track after the other boys. But the fear of lions stayed in Stephen's mind just the same.

As they started up the small rise near the water hole, Stephen felt his heart clutch nervously. He was sure they would come upon a gathering of lions, crouching there, lapping up the muddy water with their big, rough tongues.

But at the top of the crest, they stopped in surprise. Instead of lions, they saw a group of fifteen to twenty children, and two women carrying young children in their arms.

Stephen stopped in amazement. Jairo and the little boys were there, too.

But these children and women looked different from Stephen and the other boys. They were tall, or seemed so, with very long, thin legs. The women carried large, wide bowls on their heads without seeming to notice they were there.

"They are from the Shilluk tribe. A Nile tribe," Wol said. "I think. They won't hurt us. Come on. Let's get some water!"

They hurried down the hill with the sun setting at their backs.

Thirteen

Later, as he sat by the smoldering cook fire the women had started a good distance from the water hole and its dense cloud of mosquitoes, Stephen looked up at the bright desert stars, looking for Peeker and Bright Eyes, and reflected on how chance meetings changed everything.

What if they hadn't met Jairo, Henry, and Simon? And now the refugee Shilluk children and the two mothers? What if the soldiers in the plane hadn't shot the cow? They could have had milk.

Most of the younger children were sleeping. A few feet from Stephen, Wol and Jairo were playing mancala by firelight, a game of pebbles and two rows of pits hollowed out of the dirt.

The women, carrying their sleeping babies in slings of cloth, sat down by Stephen to exchange stories and talk.

"We came from a refugee camp on the Nile, north of here quite a ways," one woman said. "It got much too crowded. More than forty thousand Shilluk and Nuer people are there from all over southern Sudan."

"We came from a small village to the west of here more than six days' walking," Stephen said. "It was attacked by government soldiers. Well, we think they were northern soldiers. Jairo's village was attacked, too. All the food was stolen, and the livestock. Everyone was killed but us."

"They weren't northern government soldiers," said the older woman. "We saw them pass by here. They were southern rebels. They had loaded a truck with food sacks and household items. We even saw some children in the back. Some girls."

"Girls?" Stephen echoed. So probably the rebels had taken Naomi. "Why did they do that to us?" he asked. "Raid their own people like that?"

"For food. Money for weapons. Fighting is very expensive. They need boys, too. To become soldiers. That's probably why your mothers sent you away. That's what everyone is doing now all over Sudan, sending their sons to hide."

The older woman shrugged as though it were nothing new.

"Did you see my sister with them?" Stephen asked, then realized it was a silly question.

"How could I tell? But there were several girls in the back of the truck."

He nodded. Still, he thought that Naomi would somehow escape. Stephen was sure she would have kept a small knife tucked in the folds of her cotton dress. Naomi was strong and smart. Maybe when the soldiers got drunk or fell asleep, she would break free. He was sure of it.

"We're headed to Juba, south of the Sudd swamp-lands. There are supposed to be better supplies in the camps there near the Uganda border. So, where will you go?" the younger woman asked.

"Kenya or Ethiopia," Stephen said, trying to sound confident.

"Oh no you won't." The older woman laughed. "You can't do that anymore. They had a famine and war there, too. The refugee camps near the Ethiopian border are huge. Full. I think there are around sixty thousand people in one of them. They won't let you in. No. East of the Nile is bad right now. And Uganda camps are mostly for Acholi tribes. You are Dinka. You should go to the camps in the Central African Republic."

"Yeah? Do you think so?"

"Yes. It's best to find camps with your own tribe. It's safer. There's no way to tell who is in the camps.

There are a lot of desperate people there, that's for sure."

Stephen's stomach cramped sharply and he folded his arms, bending forward to relieve the pain. He had thought the camps would be safe, but life there sounded difficult as well. It was all too much to think about.

"Stomachache? It's the water that does that," the younger woman said. "Here. I'll give you something that will help. Not today, maybe. But in the future."

She reached into the large wide bowl she had been carrying on her head and handed Stephen two small cigarette lighters and a clay jar. "You can fill the jar with water. Then, very, very slowly, water will seep out of the bottom. The water that comes through the clay is free of mud."

Stephen stared at her as if she were a magician.

"It's true." She laughed. "And the cigarette lighters are to start a fire. Fire keeps away lions and mosquitoes. Also, fire boils water."

"Thanks!" These were wonderful presents. Stephen wanted to give the women something in return.

"Just a minute."

He went to Wol, who was still playing the pebble game, and asked for the caramel candy.

"Deng ate the candy already. Yesterday," he said.

"He is a dangerous hippopotamus who would eat anything. Now, don't bother me."

Stephen returned to the women. "I'm sorry, I have nothing to give you as a gift."

He felt dishonored by this and sat down, turning his face away slightly. They sat in silence for a while, respecting his feelings.

"Is your mother dead?" the younger woman asked.

Stephen nodded.

"And your father?"

"He's with the soldiers. I don't know where." Stephen was silent for a moment, not wanting to tell them about how he'd seen his dream father the other night. He wanted to change the subject.

"I want to go to school and become a teacher, just like the schoolteacher who came to our village last year. He had been to London once, and he told us about snow and Santa Claus."

The women smiled, just as he'd hoped.

"Listen, Stephen," said the younger one. "This year, 1999, is a very bad one in our history. Now the government has discovered oil here, and they are clearing the tribespeople from the area again. And the rebels are desperate to stop them. Maybe you should come with us south to Juba."

"And pass through the northern guards there?"

"Yes. But, you can hope . . . Not everyone is involved in this crazy war. We are Shilluk, and that's what we will do."

"We shouldn't take them," said the older woman. "The Dinka rebels are out of control in that area. The aid people in our camp told us that the Dinka shoot down international planes filled with food. They said the Dinka are destroying the Juba region. They steal food from everyone. They said that's why the aid workers don't have enough food to bring us. These boys might face capture by Dinka rebels, or revenge by Dinka enemies."

"Yes," argued the younger one. "But the Dinka only steal food to prevent the government forces from taking it all while the rest of us go hungry. Besides, it's the government who started this new war. They want to get rid of us, not the Dinka."

"Chaos is chaos. Maybe you boys could head north to the Kordofan desert," mused the older woman.

"Really?" Stephen asked in surprise. No one went north.

"There might be camps from the United Nations there," the younger woman said. "For the Nuba children. I heard that."

"Yes," said the older woman. "That's why I thought of it."

"But who knows if those villages for children really exist? I think they should come with us, south," the younger woman said.

"Take these children to the city of Juba?" asked the older woman. "Who knows what would happen to them there. We can't."

Stephen was dismayed to see that the women argued about what to do just the way the boys did. So no one knew what was best. And now he realized that only the younger woman cared about them. Not the other one. She was worried about herself.

Restlessly, Stephen got to his feet. "I don't know what we should do. Sometimes I think we should go back to our village. I'm sure that's where my sister will go if she escapes."

The women glanced at each other, but said nothing. He set the clay jar and cigarette lighters beside his backpack and began to walk away.

"Don't wander off, now," the younger woman warned.

"I won't," he said. How can I, he thought, when I don't know where to go? How can I, when there are lions waiting for me in the dark?

Fourteen

That night Stephen couldn't fall asleep, thinking about Naomi and the possibility that she had survived. He stared at the path of stars slowly moving across the sky. In the distance he heard the harsh cough of lions. With so many people in one group here and with a small fire, he didn't feel particularly scared. He didn't even care if airplanes saw their campfire. At least the smoke kept some of the mosquitoes away.

A small group of people was a good thing. But if a group of people got too big, forty thousand in one place, that wasn't good. Then fighting for food and water broke out. Stealing. Disease. Tribe against tribe. The women had told him. That was why they left the Nile camp. He didn't think they should go to Juba.

He had tried to show the women his map of Sudan, but they couldn't read or write and didn't seem to understand what it was. He was fairly sure they had already wandered too far southwest instead of south.

He watched one star moving silently in an arc across the sky. It wasn't a shooting star with a trail of dust behind it. He knew what those looked like. This was one of those magic stars that people said the Americans used to spy on the government in Sudan. He wondered if the magic star could see him lying in the dirt near the water hole with the other Sudanese children.

The moving star was gone now. He waited and waited, but he didn't see another one. He felt the coldness of night in the ground beneath him and turned on his side, pulling his knees up closer to his chest for warmth.

He was Stephen Majok, displaced person, lying on the surface of the earth, a tiny speck. He realized for the first time that the world was not simply his village, his pasture for the cows, his family, well, and hut, but a huge and strange place that he didn't understand at all.

In the morning, the cool grayness of early dawn still present in the sky overhead, Stephen woke to the sound of the other children singing a beautiful and sweet Shilluk dawn song. The women were using a long stick to stir sorghum porridge in a pot over the fire.

The Shilluk children gave Stephen, Wol, and Deng

the first bowl when it was ready. The boys devoured the warm porridge in a single minute.

Then, not knowing how else to repay their hospitality, Stephen got out his schoolbooks and drew five long lines in the dirt with a stick.

"Children!" he called out, clapping his hands just the way his teacher had. "Come in. Take your places. Smallest first."

Eagerly the kids lined up, smallest to tallest, and entered the make-believe classroom, while the two women watched.

"Good morning, class," he said.

"Good morning," the children answered loudly.

"I am your teacher, Mr. Majok. Sit down, please."

They sat on the lines in the dust.

"Welcome to school. It is sunny today. Today is letter 'D' day in English. This is letter 'D.' " He drew it in the dirt. "It says 'Duh. Duh.' "

"Duh!" the kids shouted. "Duh! Duh!"

"That's very good. But, please. Too loud. My ears," Stephen said, grabbing the sides of his head as though he had a headache.

The children smiled.

"Now, for those of you who missed class yesterday, we will review. Letter 'A' says 'a.' 'B' says 'buh.' 'C' says 'cuh' or 'sss.' 'D' says . . ."

"Duh!" the children shouted.

"Please," repeated Stephen. "Have respect for an old man's ears. Now everyone go get a stick and write these letters five times. You can count on each finger."

Later, Henry said, "You know what? You're a good teacher."

"Thanks. But who will be my teacher?"

Henry shrugged. "You have three books. Teach yourself."

Stephen tried to smile at the younger boy, but he felt tears welling up in his eyes and hurried to the edge of the group to be alone. The kids had been so excited to learn even those four letters. It was something big for them, having that school, even though it had been only a game. Stephen wiped his tears away with the palms of his hands. Why did he cry today, when things were going better?

He thought about his mother, not the way she was the last time he'd seen her, but the way she had usually been. Always, she had wanted him to learn, to go to school. She made him study every day, long after the teacher had left the village. That was the right thing, he decided.

Then he thought about what they were doing now—walking and walking, not even knowing where to go. And that seemed like the wrong thing. If he and the others made it to a camp of forty thousand people, they would soon be lost, separated from one another, from their village, from everything that they knew about.

And then, finally, he thought about Naomi. He knew if there was any way possible, she would try to make it home. Because his mother had told him to leave only until the soldiers had gone. She wouldn't want him wandering off like this.

He had to be home for Naomi. He had to wait for her there—at least for a few months. How terrible for her to escape and to find her way home only to discover that no one was there.

Stephen stood up. It was good he had cried. He felt much better now, clearer in his mind and not so much like a spinning funnel of dust blowing this way and that. He would wait for Naomi first and later decide the best way to find a school. That was what his mother would have wanted.

After washing the smallest children in the water, the women gathered some papyrus stalks growing at the edge of the water hole and boiled them with a few handfuls of beans and a speck of salt. Stephen ate his small serving of papyrus and beans, just enough to fit in his cupped hand. Then he let some clean water seep through the clay jar and licked it from the bottom. But then he was so thirsty, perhaps from the salt, that he went to the water hole and scooped up some muddy water in his jar. The women had told him to place his T-shirt over the mouth of the jar when he drank. The cloth would filter out a little mud. Stephen couldn't be bothered. He drank and drank till his stomach ached. He barely noticed the hundreds of mosquitoes swarming around his arms and legs.

For the first time in days, his head felt truly clear, his stomach somewhat full, and he looked around him at the rich golden colors of the savanna grass, the fanlike shapes of the scattered thorn trees.

He got to his feet and walked away from the water hole with his spear and stood gazing out over the wide grasslands, leaning on his spear with one leg tucked up like a stork, resting on his opposite knee and leg, the way grown men sometimes did. He had come to a decision.

Stephen straightened his shoulders and went to the two women and said for the first time, "You know that my mother is dead."

They nodded.

"And I have to honor her memory. She wanted me to learn all I could. She always said that to me. She would want me to try to find my sister."

"Yes, maybe it's wrong for you to go to these camps with no mother to watch out for you," said the older one. "There is no honor there. We lived in shame, like animals, begging for our next bowl of food, fighting and squabbling, growing sick. That's what we did for two years."

Wol and Deng came to stand with them and listen.

"But if things are uncertain, maybe we boys *should* go there, no matter what," Wol said. "What else can we do?"

The older woman thought for a moment and said, "I think now is a very bad time. There is famine and drought everywhere. The soldiers are reckless and desperate, all of them. The Nuer are your enemy. You aren't Nuer tribespeople or Shilluk. So there is possible conflict between you and the Nuer. Go to the Dinka camp in the Central African Republic. Besides this, I don't know what else to tell you."

Fifteen

Once more, the boys began to argue among themselves.

Stephen said, "You know, I think we should go home for a while until we're sure what to do. I can't go to one of those camps without knowing about Naomi. I want to go back to our village and wait there for her."

"What? How can you think she survived? She's dead, Stephen. Just like my mother and your mother and Deng's mother," Wol said angrily.

"She's dead? Then why didn't you find her body? No. I'm going. My mind is made up, Wol. I'll wait for her."

"I agree with Stephen," Deng said. "Besides, you're engaged to Naomi now. You should wait for her, too, Wol."

Wol was crying. He turned away and wiped his eyes.

"Listen, we should compromise," he said finally. "Let's go on for another three days. If we don't come to a road or some kind of aid organization, okay. We'll go home. But if we find some relief workers, we can ask them for advice. They have radios. They'll be able to tell us what to do. Then we'll at least know something definite. We can't decide based just on hope."

Stephen sighed. He didn't want to go on, but Wol's idea was probably the best one.

"Okay," he agreed. "For three days and no more."

Before they left the water hole, the women divided some of the grain they were carrying and gave the boys a small sack of sorghum. Stephen made sure that he had the clay jar with him. He put the cigarette lighters at the bottom of his pack, under his schoolbooks. As they reached the rise where the track led south, he looked back. He watched the women and children slowly moving about, gathering their things, tying them into cloth bundles. This is my life now, thought Stephen. Not playing, not herding the cows, just this wandering.

Now the six boys walked south by day instead of by night. They could move faster that way. They soon left the larger group far behind.

The track widened and became a dirt road, and they

hurried on, eager to find a village. More often, dirt tracks led out of the grasslands and joined the road. Occasionally the road rose slightly over a small rise in the land, and kites and vultures circled ceaselessly in the glazed sky. The boys saw and heard no one.

And then Jairo, who was in the front, turned around.

"Quick! A truck!" he shouted, pointing to the west. "Soldiers."

The children dashed off the road into the tall grasses.

"Stay down," Wol hissed, and the children crouched low in the grass.

"How do you know they're soldiers?" Stephen whispered to Jairo.

"I don't for sure. But we have to be safe. There wasn't time to check."

Then Stephen heard it, too. The truck engine was grinding and roaring as it bounced its way over the rough terrain. Very carefully, he peered through the tops of the grass.

Jairo was right. It was a truckload of rebel soldiers. The truck tilted sharply as it crept off a track and onto the unpaved road. It turned toward the water hole. All the soldiers standing in the back were carrying

AK-47s. Stephen glanced quickly at Henry and Simon. Their eyes were wide with fear. Henry was trying hard not to cry.

Don't let them stop. Don't let them stop, Stephen thought over and over.

"Let's stay here and rest for a while. It's okay now. Don't cry, Henry," Deng said. "They're gone."

"What about the others?" Stephen asked. "The truck is headed straight for them."

Henry began to cry in earnest.

"We have to hope they'll be able to hide in time, like we did," Deng said.

"Let's stay here a little longer," Stephen said. "I feel so tired."

The boys rested in the tall grass, until the sun's scorching heat lessened. Stephen felt himself shiver involuntarily several times. His legs and arms ached and felt heavy. He wondered how he could possibly feel this tired. He should be used to walking by now.

At last the boys got to their feet once more and picked up their belongings. Everyone took a sip of water before starting off again.

As he walked, Stephen began daydreaming about long, cool drinks of clear water. Over and over, he daydreamed the same thing. Meanwhile, his mouth got drier and drier, until his tongue felt swollen. It stuck to the roof of his mouth.

Somehow he trailed after the others all day. As the sun went down, they were still walking.

The next morning, a man in a white shirt and shorts, pushing a bicycle, joined them on the road. He told them that within one day they would come to a village where they might find some relief food and aid workers. Then he rode off like a man in a dream.

Stephen stood still, watching him grow smaller and smaller, until he vanished over a rise in the road, gone, a ghost like his father. Once again the landscape was silent and empty. Stephen swayed with dizziness. Was he dreaming while he was awake?

"Come on, Stephen," Wol said. "We made a little porridge. See? Why aren't you eating?"

"No. No, thanks. I can't," Stephen answered.

He wanted to sit down. He felt so hot and weak. He didn't understand why he was so tired. His joints ached, and the glaring sunlight seemed to make his head ring with dizziness. The glare had become a horrible buzzing in his ears. How could he ever keep walking until tomorrow?

But the other children had started walking again, and he had no choice but to follow.

By nightfall Stephen was shivering with chills that rattled his teeth. The other boys stared at him, anxiously rubbing his hands, not knowing what to do to help.

It was often cold at night, so the others covered him with their clothes and snuggled up next to him. Still he shivered. When he closed his eyes, he saw his father rise up before him, on the bicycle, now stopping and clutching his shoulder. He saw his mother lying alone in their tukel. She seemed alive and very real. He cried out in fright and confusion.

His mother sat up and stretched out her arms. She said, "I am angry, Stephen. Look how they've treated you. Look how ill and tired you are. Now I've had to come all the way back from the land of the dead. Such a long, long way I've had to come. I want to take you with me now. Come on."

"No!" Stephen shouted. "No, Mama. I'm okay here. My friends are helping me."

"Come on, Stephen. It's time to come with me."

She tugged on his arm. She shook him. He tried to wrench his arm away.

There was Deng, bending over him, squeezing his arm. "Wake up! You've had a nightmare."

Stephen forced his eyes open and sat up, trembling with cold. His teeth were chattering. His heart was pounding. His mother had seemed so real! Did the dream mean that he was going to die? He wasn't ready! This wasn't his time.

Deng stayed close, squatting beside him. "Don't cry, Stephen. We're going to get help for you soon. Please be brave a little longer. We're going to make a fire to help you stay warm, all right?"

Stephen tried to nod, but his teeth were chattering so much he wasn't able to.

Wol found one of the cigarette lighters in Stephen's pack and started a small blaze with twigs and twists of grass. The boys helped Stephen lie next to it, hoping he would stop shivering. Then the children sat close to him and put their hands on him, and that made Stephen feel a little better and less frightened. Wol heated some water and mixed it with sorghum. He gave Stephen a few sips of sorghum porridge, and when Stephen closed his eyes after that, his mother wasn't there waiting for him. Somehow he fell asleep.

The next morning dawned pale gray just before the hot sun rose. The children gathered up their things. Deng helped Stephen to stand and handed him his spear. Wol shouldered Stephen's small UN backpack, as well as his own belongings.

"He has malaria, I'm sure of it," Deng said. "From the mosquitoes. Many people in the refugee camp had it, the women said. Probably someone in the next village will have medicine."

"Okay. The others. Where are the others?" mumbled Stephen. "I don't have Peter's cow."

"What's he saying?" Henry asked.

"It's from the fever," Deng said. "He's thinking about faraway things and they feel close up."

Sixteen

Somehow, that afternoon, half carrying Stephen, the children stumbled into a village where there were three white relief aid Jeeps. Several men rushed out of their huts to help. They took Stephen to a tent that was used as a clinic, and someone went to fetch a medic.

Next to a small grass-and-mud tukel with open sides was a village church with a canvas roof propped up by poles. Stephen could see the cross set up in the open-air tent. Was this a Catholic village? Weren't northern Muslims trying to kill Catholics? Maybe this was a dangerous place. For a moment, he looked around in confusion.

"Are there soldiers?" he asked. "We can't stay here!"

"Lie down now, Stephen," Deng said. "Just rest."

Stephen tumbled onto a cot draped with mosquito netting. Henry and Simon stood near his cot while they waited for someone to come.

Deng noticed a pail of water on a table and brought Stephen a ladleful. He sipped a few drops, then lay back again, exhausted from the work of swallowing.

Finally an aid worker came and examined him, feeling his throat and under his arms, looking into his mouth and eyes. "Stephen? My name is Charles. Now I'm going to clean your face a little with some cool water," the medic said.

"Will he be okay?" Wol asked. "What's wrong with him?"

"He has malaria. That's a disease carried by mosquitoes. If he takes the medicine regularly for two weeks, he should recover pretty well. But he is malnourished and dehydrated, too. No doubt you all are. How long have you been walking?"

The children looked at one another. No one knew exactly.

"More than a month?" Charles asked.

"Oh, no. A week. No. Longer than that. More like ten or eleven days," Wol answered. "Soldiers came and burned our villages, so we left. They took everything—cows, grain, tools—and killed nearly everyone."

"And where are you going?"

"I . . . we . . ." Wol began. "To Juba. Or Kenya. Actually, we don't know."

"Can we have some water now?" Henry asked, tugging on the man's shorts to get his attention.

"Certainly. We have a good well. Here, take the pail. It's nearly empty. The well is there, in front of the church. You can draw the water yourselves."

Charles sat down at the table for a moment and wrote something. Then he went to a locked metal cabinet and opened it, taking out a brown glass bottle, while the boys watched.

"Are you Sudanese? Are you from the Acholi tribe, maybe?" Wol asked, picking up the pail.

"No. I'm a medically trained aid worker from Kenya."

"Wol, can we go for the water now?" Henry asked.

"No," said Wol. "Wait just a minute. I want to make sure Stephen is okay first."

After cleaning Stephen's arms and face of caked-on dust and dry sweat, and laying a cold compress on his hot forehead, Charles said, "I'm going to give you your first dose of medicine now, Stephen. Sit up just a little. That's it."

But Stephen's whole body was shaking. The spoon rattled against his teeth. The medicine spilled on his chest.

"That's all right. Let's try it again," Charles said patiently. "You'll get it this time."

After swallowing the medicine and a few sips of

sweet, milky tea, Stephen lay back and fell into a fever-ish sleep.

During his fever spells, Stephen continued to have strange dreams, vivid and seeming very real. He saw his father many times. And his mother, whom no one had buried. And he saw his sister, Naomi. She was calling for him to come home, to plant the crops and gather firewood for charcoal. Stephen wanted desperately to talk to her.

"Wait!" he called out. "Naomi, wait for me." Was it Naomi who was now coming for him from the Land of the Dead and not his mother? Had he made a terrible mistake?

When he woke up, he forgot that he was covered with mosquito netting, and fought with it, thinking it was biting ants, tearing it off his face before he realized what he was doing.

"It's okay, Stephen. Just relax."

Stephen focused his eyes on the unknown face. Even looking at something felt like hard work, and he didn't remember seeing this man before at all.

"Who are you?" he asked.

"My name is Charles. From Kenya. I am working with Norwegian People's Aid here in Sudan. This is a small relief aid depot."

"Kenya? Are there really mountains with snow on them there?" Stephen asked.

"Yes."

"And how does snow taste?" Stephen said. "Is it sweet?"

Charles laughed. "I don't know. I never ate any."

"But I don't . . . where are . . . where . . . ?" Stephen again began pulling at the netting, trying to get up.

"Lie down," Charles said firmly. "Your friends are here. You need to be a lot stronger than this before you get up."

Stephen nodded. Exhaustion swept through him like a gust of hot wind. He lay down. Charles carefully re-arranged the netting around the cot.

"Let's not let any mosquitoes come in to visit you for a few more days. All right?"

Stephen smiled, too tired to speak.

Seventeen

The next day the other group of children, accompanied by the two women, arrived in the village. They, too, had managed to hide from the truckload of soldiers. Charles sat beside Stephen and told him that he had arranged for them to go to a camp near Juba by bus.

And a few days later, the Shilluk were taken in a beat-up old bus to a refugee camp on the road to Juba. Before they left, Charles tried to persuade the women to take the other children as well—Deng and Wol, Henry and Simon. But only Jairo, who as the oldest was most terrified of being caught by soldiers, went with them. Henry and Simon refused to leave, struggling and hollering until they were allowed to stay behind with Deng and Wol, to wait for Stephen to get better.

By taking the medicine day after day, Stephen did feel better. There was less aching in his bones. His terrible dreams stopped. His headache lessened. He was able to sit up and eat some sorghum porridge twice a day.

He began to notice things again, and to look out from the open sides of the tent at the dusty and mostly deserted village around him. Little things—a passing butterfly, the shifting shape of afternoon clouds— seemed precious to him, like something he had almost lost but now had the chance to see again.

The relief center was made up of several large sheds constructed of corrugated tin, which were full of bags of grain, and there were three Jeeps and a priest with pale pink skin and reddish hair. He was funny-looking. There were also stacks of tires and several old truck engines under one of the trees. The priest spent a lot of time with a Sudanese man who was trying to repair one of the Jeeps.

But even sitting up like this for a few minutes made Stephen extremely tired.

One day a lot of trucks and Jeeps and two crazily painted old buses came and picked up some of the aid workers, then went away. That day, Stephen had his fever again, and he couldn't make sense of what he saw.

Despite afternoons when his fever returned, he kept getting better, slowly but surely. Charles had a short-wave radio run by batteries. At night, he sat next to Stephen's cot and pulled up the antenna, and they listened to the fuzzy, scratchy squeaking of faraway radio stations: Moscow, Chicago, London, Cairo, Rome, Tel Aviv. Thrilled and curious, Stephen pulled out his geography book, and together they found each city. He decided then and there that he wanted to be a geography teacher.

Charles could read and write in English, and as Stephen's headache disappeared, he began to teach him some vocabulary and grammar. He also taught him English numbers and how to count beyond twenty. Stephen asked Charles about the magic stars that passed overhead at night. Charles said they were called satellites. They were not airplanes, but they were more like airplanes than real stars, and many of them were for communications, sending and receiving radio waves.

"What are radio waves?" Stephen asked, picking up the radio and examining the back of it to see if it contained any hidden tricks. "How do the voices get inside this radio?" Mystified, Stephen turned the radio over and over in his hands. "There can't be tiny people inside it, talking to us in every language, can there?"

Charles tried to explain that radio waves were waves of electricity that invisibly traveled through air. The sounds were made by radio waves sent by satellite. The radio had a device inside it to receive them.

But Stephen couldn't understand how that worked. Or how he had seen tiny people on the television set that the teacher had once brought to the village.

After three weeks, when Stephen was strong enough to walk around the village without help, Charles said, "I'm sorry to tell you this. You boys can't stay here any longer. There are no families staying here. We can't allow it. Just the priest, who is from Norway, stays, and some aid workers like me, and some men who work on repairing the aid trucks. That's all."

"But why can't we stay? We haven't bothered anybody," Wol said.

"You see those sheds at the edge of the village? Sometimes we get large deliveries of food here for distribution to camps to the south. And then, when there is food here, the soldiers come and raid the place. It wouldn't be safe for you. They'd try to make you go with them and become soldiers, too."

Stephen glared angrily at his new friend for telling them they should leave. He had trusted Charles until now, and thought of him as fondly as he did his old teacher from last year. Now Charles was telling them they had to go. He knew they would leave for home, but he couldn't stand being told to go. He couldn't stand feeling rejected in any way. He hated Charles fiercely at that moment.

"Come on," Stephen muttered to the others. He walked off angrily.

The boys sat in the shade of a large baobab tree behind the church hut, trying to decide what to do.

"While I was sick," Stephen said, "I had many dreams about our old village. My sister, Naomi, my father, my mother—they were all telling me to come home. These are my relatives speaking. Not foreigners like Charles, aid people who come and go. My mother should be honored."

"Of course we'll go back for Naomi," said Wol finally. "Probably it's just as safe to go back as to go on to places we don't know. The bus driver said the swamps are five to eight days' walking. What if we got lost in the swamps?"

No one spoke as they considered this. "We don't know anything about those swamps or how to survive there," Stephen said.

"I like to eat fish, though," Deng said.

Stephen grinned and pushed him lightly on the arm. "And crocodiles would like to eat you!" he said. "Yum!"

"I don't know how to swim," said Henry.

"Me neither," said little Simon. "If those swamp rivers are wide and deep, I'll drown trying to get across."

Stephen wasn't sure he could swim well enough to cross a large river, either. He lay on his back and gazed up into the many branches of the baobab and, beyond them, the bright blue sky. "Soon it will be the middle of the rainy season. What if they've had rain in that region? Those rivers will grow wider and wider," he said.

"Maybe it has even rained at home. When it rains, the wells will fill up," said Deng. "Easier to get water for drinking, and we won't have to irrigate the crops for weeks and weeks."

Stephen sat up and looked at his friend. "You're right. We're farmers," he said. "That's how we can survive. The crops are planted already. How is it we never thought of this before?"

Everyone thought back to their horror when they had entered the village and seen what they had seen, how they had fled panic-stricken into the woods, thinking of nothing but escape.

Stephen sighed. "So, it's decided. We're going back, as Wol said."

Wol nodded. The boys fell silent, thinking of the hardships they had gone through on their way to this place—the low-flying airplanes, the terrible thirst, the muddy water, the mosquitoes and Stephen's malaria, the truckload of soldiers, the fear of lions at night.

"We don't have a rope," said Wol finally. "For the well. Remember? The soldiers took it. We can't make any mistakes. We'll need a rope."

"And a bucket. Some grain and beans for replanting in case the crops have died," Deng said.

"And a knife," said Stephen.

"No," said Wol. "Not a knife, a machete."

"Both," said Stephen. "And sorghum and my medicine. Maybe Charles will drive us back to the water hole. By truck, it can't be far. Maybe half a day."

"Are you crazy? Stop thinking about that guy. Will he let us take those things we need? No. Probably not," Wol said. "And besides, what if we meet soldiers? We won't be able to hide if we're on a truck."

Suddenly, thought Stephen, Wol was full of ideas and energy. Well, that was good. He was relieved because he still felt tired, even from something as simple as talking.

"Okay. Anyway, going home is never as hard as leaving," Stephen said to reassure the others, though he wondered how he would ever make it back.

"But we won't tell a soul that we're going," Wol said, and he made the boys all swear to secrecy.

That night, while Stephen was resting in the tent, listening to Radio Cairo, Wol and Henry entered one of the large storage sheds and stole a bucket, a long coil of rope, grain, and some beans. They put the grain and beans in the bucket and tiptoed out again. Simon's job was to fill the goatskin water bag and bottles at the well.

Stephen's job was to wait until Charles went to bed and then take several bottles of malaria medicine from the white metal cabinet. Then he stuffed his mosquito netting into his UN pack and made sure he had his books, the clay jar, and the two cigarette lighters.

Then they all met behind the huge trunk of the baobab. Overhead, the stars blazed brightly. The Milky Way looked like a spray of foam across the sky.

"I think we should leave at once," Wol said. "We should travel at night as much as possible again, at least as far as the water hole. Night travel is safer."

"Why?" asked Deng. "Who would come after us?"

"I don't know," Wol said. "But no one needs to know which way we went. Let them think we headed south, like the others."

"I still want to say goodbye to Charles," Stephen said. "It's wrong just to sneak out on him."

"No!" Wol said.

"Yes. He saved my life. I want to thank him."

"Are you crazy? Come on. What if he tries to stop us from going back? What if they kidnap us, lock us up, and deliver us to soldiers for money or something?"

"Charles would never do that!" Stephen argued.

"How do you know?"

"Will you two shut up?" Deng said. "We should go, Stephen. Wol is right. Charles will understand."

Stubbornly, Stephen turned to the two little boys to see what they thought. "We should go," Simon said. Henry nodded.

"Okay," Stephen muttered. All at once he felt tired and rubbed his forehead, which was covered with prickly sweat.

They picked up their belongings. Stephen had only his pack and the clay jar to carry, but they felt heavy before he had even left the village.

They had walked about twenty minutes when Wol stopped in the center of the starlit road and said, "I forgot the machete."

"Never mind, Wol," Deng said. "It's not worth worrying about."

"Yes it is. I'm going back for it."

"What? You wouldn't let me say goodbye to Charles and now you're going back for a machete?" Stephen shouted.

"Ssssh! You know your mistake, Stephen? All you

care about is people. Well, I don't. People can hurt you. But a machete can save your life," Wol said proudly.

Deng groaned. "Stephen, Wol, calm down. Okay? Already we're arguing again, and we've barely started back," he said. "Wol, don't argue with Stephen. Leave him alone."

"Fine!"

Wol turned around, and with long strides, he marched off in the direction of the village. The other boys sat down in the tall grass to wait.

Eighteen

Ten days or more had passed when, as they finally neared their village, Stephen stopped in his tracks and sniffed. He smelled a trace of smoke. Woodsmoke.

Had the soldiers returned to his village after destroying everything? What could be on fire now? What could possibly be left to burn?

His heart began to pound with fear as he peered out of the edge of dense brush across the pasture where once he'd tended the cows. He gestured for the others to crouch down.

"What's wrong?" hissed Wol.

"Smoke."

"Are there people there, Stephen?" asked Henry. "Bad people?"

"Ssssh! We'll have to wait here until we figure out what to do," Stephen said.

"I'm not waiting. I'm going closer," Wol said. He pulled the machete out of his bundle.

"One boy attacking an unknown enemy?" Deng muttered in disgust. "Do you expect us to rush in and rescue you?"

Wol didn't answer. He grasped the handle of the machete more tightly. Slowly he crept through the tall grass toward the remains of the village.

Stephen could see that his and old Garang's tukels were still among the few standing. Wol headed toward the destroyed village and Stephen's hut. Anxiously watching from the safety of the trees, twisting his fingers while he waited, Stephen wondered if some villagers had been spared or had escaped and had now returned, just as the boys were returning. Either that, or some other displaced villagers had stopped here, perhaps because of the well.

At that moment, the boys saw Wol jump up. He leaped high into the air like a dancer celebrating, like a gazelle!

"Come on!" yelled Stephen.

The boys ran through the grass.

"Who is it?" called Stephen. "Who's there?"

"Naomi!" cried Wol over his shoulder. "I saw her enter your hut!"

Whooping and leaping, the boys raced toward the

circle of burned huts. A cook fire was smoking in the doorway to the Majoks' tukel.

"Naomi! Naomi!" Stephen cried.

There she was! In the doorway to their tukel. His frightened sister stared at the boys, poised to run at any moment.

"Oh, Stephen! It *is* you! I wasn't sure!" she cried.

They hugged each other. "What? How could you not recognize me?" he asked.

"You're so thin. Look at your ribs! And Wol!" They hugged tightly. "And Deng, too! Oh, Stephen, it's been so terrible here since the attack. The soldiers took me in a truck. They beat me and said they would sell me in Khartoum, that wealthy Muslims would buy me as a slave."

"How did you get away?"

"They had only tied my hands behind my back. So, on the second night, I waited till they were all drunk and snoring, and then I started walking."

"The ropes were still tied?" Stephen asked.

"Yes. See? I still have scabs on my wrists from where they were bleeding. Anyway, I walked and walked like that, looking for a hiding place. And then I hid in some bushes for about three days, until I was so hungry and thirsty I had to start back to the village or die. And finally I got here and Peter Garang cut the ropes. And when I came inside the tukel, then I found Mama," she ended in a low voice. "I didn't know why you weren't here. Didn't you hear Mama say to come back here as soon as possible?"

"I did come back! We all did, didn't we, Wol? But no one was here."

"Is anyone else here now?" Deng asked.

"Garang and his first wife were here, but they left. They probably survived by informing. And there were several others—older people. But they all left, too. All the cows are gone. In the whole village, there are only two goats."

Stephen sank to the ground, feeling overwhelmed and dizzy with relief. What if they hadn't returned? What if they'd gone on to Juba in the bus?

It seemed almost an accident, no, a miracle, that they had found Naomi again. That was a terrible thing about war. There was no way to know what was the right thing to do—whom to trust, where to go. He could have lost Naomi forever, and she him.

"Come on. Let's go in," said Stephen to the little boys, crouching next to him. "You can stay here in our tukel."

The boys ducked inside and huddled together on the mats. Henry and Simon were crying now, thinking of their home. Deng lay down on a mat, too, and turned to face the wall, grieving once again that he had no one in his family to be with.

Naomi approached Wol and took his hands.

"Wol, I'm glad you came back for me. That was brave of you."

"It was brave of me, too," Stephen said, feeling a little jealous.

"Of course!" Naomi laughed. "Now. Are you boys hungry?" she asked. She smiled at Henry and Simon, trying to make them feel welcome.

They nodded.

"I'm sure Deng is hungry, too," Stephen said. "He's always ready to eat."

Naomi turned to Stephen. "I've been collecting grain and rice from the ground of the burned huts, picking kernels out of the dirt. The soldiers spilled some in their hurry. But it's not much. We'll all have to work hard in the fields. We'll have to carry water by hand. It's only rained once, for less than an hour. The ground soaked it up as fast as it came down."

But Stephen could barely listen. He kept glancing at the spot where he'd last seen his mother, lying on the ground.

"What about Mama?" he asked. "What did you . . . ?"

Naomi turned away. "I buried her ages ago."

"By yourself?"

"Yes. I had to." Then she changed the subject. "You know what? I let the goats sleep in here with me."

"Really?" Stephen smiled through his grief.

"So. Now I'll make some kisra bread for you," said Naomi. "There's water in the calabash. Give some to the two little boys."

Stephen handed Henry the heavy gourd of water and then went out and squatted at the entrance to the hut, by the cook fire, beside his sister and Wol.

"How did you get water?" Stephen asked. "The soldiers took the rope from the well."

"Yes. I cut up some cloth strips and tied them together," Naomi said.

"Wol brought a rope, so we can replace that tomorrow. But, Naomi, we almost didn't come back here at all. We were going to try to reach a refugee camp someplace," he said.

Naomi slapped the sorghum paste into a flat pancake shape and laid it on the pan. She shook her head, probably thinking of what this would have meant, but didn't speak.

"Where is Mama's grave?" Stephen asked in a low voice.

"We'll go there later," she said.

"Tell me the truth, Naomi. Are we safe here?" asked Stephen.

"I don't know. But I think that for now the soldiers won't come back. Why should they? There's nothing here for them. No cows, nothing to steal. So maybe through this rainy season, we'll be okay. The village is probably as safe as anywhere. That's what I tell myself when I'm scared. But I think we should leave." She glanced at Stephen. "When everyone is strong again."

"We'll have to go to the Central African Republic," Wol said. "And find a camp there. We won't try to make it through the swamps. Naomi, about us, do you think we should get married now?"

Naomi sat back on her heels, thinking. "No. We should wait. When we reach the camp and are settled there, that's when we should talk about it."

"That's good," said Wol, sounding relieved. "When we leave, Stephen, we have to be better prepared this time. We'll need to study your map."

"Stephen will have to go to school there, Wol," Naomi said.

"Yes. We know. He bothers us about this every day."

"Well, yeah. Not every day. But almost." Stephen grinned. "Can we eat now?"

The smell of the hot bread was making his stomach growl. Naomi heard it and smiled. Stephen laid his head on her shoulder.

"Here. Take this in and serve the little ones first."

Stephen took the kisra bread into the hut. He tore the steaming piece in two and gave half to Henry and Simon. The other piece he gave to Deng.

"Are we safe here, Stephen? Did Naomi say so?" Henry asked. "Did you ask her?"

"We'll stay here through the rainy season," Stephen said, glad he had something to tell them. He sat down by Deng. "Then we'll decide. For now, Naomi and I will be your family," he said.

The little boys smiled, and Deng nodded. "I know you will. And for you, I'd do the same."

"Come on, Deng," said Stephen, "eat this bread. It's warm. And drink all you want. The water here is pure."